The Land of Delights

The Land of Delights:
Tales of Enchantments

by
**Charlotte-Rose
Caumont de La Force**

Translated, annotated and introduced by
Brian Stableford

A Black Coat Press Book

Visit our website at www.blackcoatpress.com

ISBN 978-1-61227-760-8. First Printing. July 2018. Published by Black Coat Press, an imprint of Hollywood Comics.com, LLC, P.O. Box 17270, Encino, CA 91416. All rights reserved. Except for review purposes, no part of this book may be reproduced or transmitted in any form or by any means, electronic or mechanical, including photocopying, recording, or by any information storage and retrieval system, without permission in writing from the publisher. The stories and characters depicted in this novel are entirely fictional. Printed in the United States of America.

TABLE OF CONTENTS

Introduction

Les Contes des Contes[1] bearing the signature Mademoiselle de ***, was originally printed in Paris, under a royal license dated 27 July 1697, in two volumes, by Simon Bernard. The title-page of the book bears the date 1698, but a subsequent note claims that the print-run was actually completed on 23 December 1697. The eight tales were reissued in 1707, by two different printers, as *Les Fées, contes des contes par Rose de Caumont de La Force*, thus being attributed to Charlotte-Rose Caumont de La Force (1650-1724). They were reprinted again in 1725, attributed to "Mademoiselle de ***," and were then attributed to "Mademoiselle de La Force" when they were included in the one of the 1785 volumes of *Le Cabinet des fées ou Collection choisie des contes de fées et autres contes merveilleux*, a huge assembly falsely represented as being published in Amsterdam or Geneva (because books legally printed in pre-Revolutionary Paris still required a royal license, which their publisher did not have).

By the time the collection was first printed, as part of a rapid flood of such publications prompted by the commercial success of Charles Perrault's collection of tales, *Contes de ma mère l'Oye* (1697; tr. as "Tales of Mother Goose"), Mademoiselle de La Force was no

---

[1] As the printer's note points out, this title [literally, The Tales of Tales], was invented by him, not supplied by the author, and the immodest implication that they are the best or most archetypal of their species was not hers.

longer at Louis XIV's court. She had been banished therefrom earlier in 1697, the king having threatened to rescind the pension that he had previously granted her— her only substantial means of support—if she did not retire to Benedictine abbey of Gercy, in Brie, where she remained for the next sixteen years. The reasons for her expulsion remain profoundly unclear. There was talk of scandal, but scandal was rife at the court, and any specific charges laid against her are highly likely to have been trumped up. At any rate, she protested her innocence vehemently, and it is now impossible to discover the truth. She had made her debut in the court in 1666, initially serving as one of the queen's maids-of-honor, and there were many posthumous allegations about various affairs that she might have had during the next thirty years, including a widely-reported secret marriage to the actor Charles Briou, but none of them can be substantiated and all of them are probably best dismissed as malicious gossip and fabrication. What is certain is that, having been raised as a Protestant, she converted to Catholicism in 1686, after the Edict of Nantes, and any backsliding on that diplomatic move would probably have been adequate to occasion the particular condemnation that she received.

In all probability, all of the stories in *Les Contes de Contes* had been composed before her banishment, some of them several years before, but if the last of them, "La Bonne Femme" (tr. as "The Good Woman") was not written at Gercy, it might be reckoned an intriguing anticipation of the sentiments associated with her exile. By far the most famous of the tales, from the viewpoint of the present day, is "Persinette," for the ironic reason that it was plagiarized by Friedrich Schultz, who represented it falsely as a German folktale, having retitled it "Rapunzel" (1790), and it was subsequently collected under that title by the Brothers Grimm. The Grimm version was very widely reprinted, and still gets the credit for subsequent transformations of the story, including the recent Disney film *Tangled* (2010). Mademoiselle de La Force had borrowed the key elements of the story, including the striking motif of the captive princess letting down her hair in order that the prince can climb up to her prison, from "Petrosinella," in Giambattista Basile's collection of fanciful tales usually known as *Il Pentamerone* (1634-36; Fr. tr. 1672), which provided a rich source of inspiration for the tales reformulated by the storytellers of the salons of Louis XIV's court. Her version is, however, considerably elaborated, and its plaintive later phases are markedly different from Basile's story.

The author was already well-known before her collection of tales of enchantment appeared, having recently issued several books in the popular gene of "secret histories," supposedly factual accounts of the lives of long-dead famous individuals "revealing" unpublished, and usually scandalous, details of their private lives, some doubtless based in anecdotal gossip and the rest invented. Her principal publications in that genre were *Histoire secrète de Marie de Bourgogne* (1694; the "Marie de" was dropped in subsequent editions), *Histoire secrète des amours de Henri IV, roi de Castille, surnommé l'Impuissant* (1695) and *Histoire de Marguerite de Valois, reine de Navarre, soeur de François Ier* (1696). She published the novel *Histoire de Gustave Vasa de Suède* in 1697-98, and added two further volumes to the set of secret histories in the first two decades of the eighteenth century.[2]

Long after her death, in 1865, another work by Mademoiselle de La Force was published as *Les Jeux d'esprit, ou la Promenade de la princesse de Conti à Eu*, written in 1701, which belongs to a different genre, being an account of imaginary conversations supposedly taking place in the second decade of the seventeenth century between the then Princesse de Conti[3] and a number of her friends, which includes accounts of various fantastic dreams—for which the members of the company attribute speculative psychological interpretations—improvised commentaries on the "metamorphoses" of perceived objects, and invented historical fictions. That volume has an introduction by Édouard Lelièvre, Marquis de La Grange, which explains how the manuscript turned up when Louis-Philippe's book collection was sold at auction in 1852, and also includes a previously-unpublished account of the author written by herself and

---

[2] All of Mademoiselle de La Force's works are summarized at great length by Joseph La Porte in his invaluable *Histoire littéraire des femmes françaises* (1769), which can be read on Google Books.

[3] The Princesse de Conti featured in the story is Louise Marguerite de Lorraine (1588-1631), but it is very probable that the person La Force actually had in mind was Marie-Thérèse de Bourbon (1666-1732), wife of François-Louis de Bourbon, who appears to have been La Force's principal protectress at the court, at least to begin with. There was another Princesse de Conti at court at the time, Marie-Anne de Bourbon (1666-1739), who was the same age, but she was known as the dowager Princesse after her husband, Louis-Armand de Bourbon, the elder brother of his successor, died in 1685.

addressed to the Prince de Conti (François-Louis de Bourbon, 1664-1709).

The flippantly immodest account in question contains such remarks as "I am entirely the enemy of constraint, and yet all my life is a perpetual constraint" and "I was born independent and haughty, loving glory to the point of excess." She claims that "my life is a continual philosophy and a living morality" and that "Exact in my virtue, I nevertheless forgive willingly faults that only others have." She also asserts, that: "I have a very tender heart. I have always been deceived, and only found in my entire life one good *amie* [female friend]; I have had perfidious and false friends in quantity" and that "No one ever had a soul so passionate." All of that doubtless has to be taken with a pinch of salt, but it does cast some light on the psychology of the tales, which are markedly different from those of Marie-Jeanne de l'Héritier de Villandon (1664-1734),[4] the chief promoter of the salon fashion for improvising such concoctions, and Madame d'Aulnoy, who became the most prolific and the best-known author of written versions thereof.

The printer's note makes it clear that it was him, and not Mademoiselle de La Force, who wanted to rush the collection into print, in an attempt to cash in on the success of Perrault's collection. Mademoiselle L'Héritier had already published some of her tales in that vein in a collection of her miscellaneous works, so Mademoiselle de La Force, and Madame d'Aulnoy, along with the Comtesse de Murat—all three of whom had already made a name with secret histories—were undoubtedly

---

[4] See *The Robe of Sincerity*, Black Coat Press, ISBN 978-1-61227-732-5.

the primary targets for such entrepreneurial endeavor in the marketing of what came to be known as *contes de fées* [tales of enchantment, but usually mistranslated as "fairy tales"].[5]

Because Perrault reaped the lion's share of the celebrity subsequently associated with that popularization—only shared to any considerable extent with Madame d'Aulnoy—some subsequent historians suggested that Mademoiselle de L'Héritier, who was his distant cousin, got the idea of writing such tales from him, but it was almost certainly the other way around; Perrault seems to have appropriated some of her tentative pioneering materials, along with materials from the other female writers involved in the salon fad.

Because of the second-stage popularization of *contes de fées*, which shaped and marketed the material specifically as tales to be read to children, the origins of the vogue in the salons of Versailles and Paris have been obscured, and the whole picture is impossible to reconstitute, but certain aspects of it can still be vaguely discerned. Its primary nucleus was the salon hosted by Madeleine de Scudéry (1607-1701), who had carried forward a tradition originated in the salon hosted at the Hôtel de Rambouillet by Catherine de Vivonne, Marquise de Rambouillet (1588-1665) from 1608 until her

---

[5] The French *féerie* means "enchantment," so a *fée* is, literally, an agent of enchantment. Because the noun has the feminine gender, however, it is frequently assumed that the agents in question are female, and the word has a masculine equivalent in *enchanteur*. It is perfectly clear in Mademoiselle de La Force's stories, as it is in Mademoiselle de L'Héritier's, that her *fées* are human enchantresses, not supernatural beings, as is implied by the English word "fairies." It is for that reason that I invariably translate *fée* as "fay."

death. The primitive feminism of their salons was paro-
died by Molière in the brief farce "Les Précieuses ridi-
cules" [The Ridiculous Precious Women] (1659)—as a
result of which the key salon members became known as
the *précieuses*—and "Les Femmes savantes" [The Sa-
vant Women] (1672), after Mademoiselle de Scudéry
had become the most popular writer in France (although
her works were published under her brother's name),
effectively kick-starting the commercial publication of
fiction and laying the groundwork for the modern novel.

The books that obtained that unprecedented popu-
larity reached their peak of achievement and celebrity in
the ten-volume *Artamène, ou le Grand Cyrus* (1649-
1653) and the ten-volume *Clélie, histoire romaine*
(1654-1660), which were, in effect, serials, ancestral in
their narrative technique and concerns to modern TV
soap operas. They also pioneered the strategy of the *ro-
man à clef*, in which contemporary individuals are dis-
guised as fictional characters, in these cases in the context of a Classical pseudohistory. The *précieuses* not
only did that in their literary works but in their conversation too, frequently referring to their contemporaries by
pseudonyms, partly to mask salacious gossip and mock-
ery. It is now impossible to judge the extent to which the
characters featured in the fanciful tales improvised in the
salons, often in a fashion similar to the games described
by La Force in *Les Jeux d'Esprit*, are parodies of actual
individuals at Louis XIV's court, but what is certain is
that the fictitious world of fays, princes and princesses
featured in the stories, and its social conventions and

mores, is a distorted image of European—and, essentially, Parisian—high society in the age of Louis XIV.[6]

Because the myth that *contes de fées* were based on folktales has gained such currency, it has become easy to overlook or forget that they were originally addressed to a purely aristocratic audience, and that they address concerns, both overtly and covertly, that were primarily and essentially of interest to that audience. Their sources are not folkloristic at all, but purely literary; Mademoiselle de L'Héritier, the movement's principal theorist, contended that the tales that she and her friends were imitating had only become stories handed down over the generations after initially being composed by Provençal troubadours for recitation in the courts of the twelfth and thirteenth century, specifically addressed to feudal aristocrats, partly for the purpose of glorification and partly by way of diplomatically-veiled criticism. Whether that is strictly true is debatable, but there is no doubt at all that that is what the members of L'Héritier's coterie believed and thought they were doing in their own *jeux d'esprit* in Mademoiselle de Scudéry's salon; Mademoiselle de La Force's stories are very obviously written with that theory in mind. When the salon storytellers borrowed from Basile, it was not because they thought that Basile's stories were based in Italian folklore (a highly dubious contention) but because they recognized a similarity between their content and the notion of

---

[6] A more elaborate account of the "prehistory" of *contes de fées* and the importance of Mademoiselle de Scudéry as a precursor can be found in the introduction to the Black Coat Press edition of Mademoiselle de l'Héritier's tales, *The Robe of Sincerity*, q.v.

"troubadour romances" promoted by L'Héritier and endorsed by Scudéry.

Even though she is no longer read, it is arguable that Mademoiselle de Scudéry was the single most influential figure in the entire history of European literature, partly because of the crucial influences her works had on the subsequent development of prose fiction, its obsessions—particularly its obsession with the politics of amour—and its marketing, but also because of her furtherance and perfection of the salon tradition that she inherited from the Marquise de Rambouillet. In addition to her fiction and her poetry, Scudéry was a prolific writer of non-fiction, a great deal of which was devoted to the art of conversation, and the application of classical analyses of rhetoric and eloquence to contemporary oral and written discourse. She not only inherited from her predecessor the idea that the principal focal point of salon conversation should be literature, but she attempted to dictate how that conversation should be organized and conducted; she made her salon into a literary workshop, in which she sought to define what the works produced by its members ought to be attempting to contrive, and she strove to establish rules for their discussion and evaluation. As with the modern literary mythology of "romance," a direct line of descent connects Scudéry's endeavors with modern writing workshops; she was the ancestress not only of the subsequent evolution of French literary salons and Romantic cenacles, but of their English and American spinoff, and thus played a crucial role in the development of countless cauldrons of subsequent literary inspiration.

The importance of the latter point, in respect of the emergence from Scudéry's salon of *contes de fées*, is that the process of that emergence was entirely conscious, strategically contrived in the context of a particular view of literary endeavor. There is, obviously, no record of the conversations that took place in the salon and its various clones, and their echoes in such literary works as *Les Jeux d'Esprit* are dramatically transfigured, but the tales themselves tell a story—a *conte des contes*, if you wish—that is very different from the historical fantasy that has been built on Perrault's adaptation of them as moralistic tales for reading to children. Moralistic they certainly are, but the morals attached to Mademoiselle de La Force's tales are certainly not aimed at children. In fact, what distinguishes her tales from those of her most famous contemporaries is their evident moral unease, which sometimes extends to outright challenge, as in the remarkable rant in the conclusion to "La Puissance d'Amour" (tr. as "The Power of Amour"). Although the bare bones of "Persinette" have survived as a children's story it is only by adaptation, and it is significant that the only other tale of La Force's that has had any considerable recirculation as a "fairy story" is "Plus Belle que Fée" (tr. here as "More Beautiful than a Fay," but known in other versions as "Fairer-than-a-Fairy"), also in a simplified version.

One of the most celebrated products of the *précieuses*, popularized in its own day by an engraving in the first volume of *Clélie*, was the allegorical *Carte du Tendre* [Map of Tenderness], which supposedly charted the reliable path to true love. Mademoiselle de La Force produced her own allegory of that sort in "Le Pays des délices" (tr. as "The Land of Delights"), but a comparison of the imaginary geographies and the journey that they map out illustrates very clearly that La Force is possessed of a far greater skepticism than her mentor, and that her notion of Amour and the route to its attainment is far less rose-tinted. That contention is graphically symbolized in "Tourbillon" as well as "La Puissance d'Amour," and is developed with telling elaboration in both "Vert et bleu" (tr. as "Green and Blue"), another story in which jealousy functions as a brutal plot-lever, and the bizarre emotional roller-coaster plot of "L'Enchanteur" (tr. as "The Enchanter"). All eight stories, in fact, give evidence of the same painful existential wounds that led the author to say of herself, in her self-portrait that "I have always been deceived, and only found in my entire life one good friend; I have had perfidious and false friends in quantity..."[7]

Of all the pioneering writers of *contes de fées*, La Force is perhaps the one who took the greatest imaginative license from the freedom to make arbitrary inventions and narrative moves. Although far less prolific than Madame d'Aulnoy, and therefore less various in the motifs that she adopted and deployed, her stories are usually longer than d'Aulnoy's, and thus more elaborate in their development. Although by no means lacking in focus, they routinely follow strange narrative trajectories that give them an almost surreal quality. It is not surprising that the one existing tale that she admittedly adapted for her own purposes was the bizarrely enigmatic English romance of *Sir Gawain and the Green Knight*, which

---

[7] We can only speculate as to who that one *amie* was; perhaps the most likely candidate is the Princesse de Conti, but one is tempted at least to wonder whether it might have been Mademoiselle de L'Héritier. It cannot have been Baronne d'Aulnoy, who was banished from the court for a long time, for scandalous conduct, although she was readmitted in 1690, nor La Force's young cousin, the Comtesse de Murat, who was to follow her into banishment in 1702 following a scandal that first broke in 1699.

must have appealed to her fondness for the absurd in the same way as the roles played by a craving for parsley and exceedingly long hair in "Petrosinella."

Although the style of Mademoiselle de La Force's writing is a trifle stilted—understandably, in view of its antiquity—and she has certain idiosyncratic quirks, especially her liking for rapid synoptic explanations contained in long sentences replete with semi-colons, which occasionally inhibit ready comprehension, her cavalier plotting and the zest with which she develops her motifs often seem to be ahead of their time, and quite modern in their wry black-edged humor. Her works are certainly best read as a set, and in the order in which they were originally presented, which was presumably determined by the author rather than the printer who chivvied her into letting him strike while the iron of demand was hot. As with most such collections, hers is greater than the sum of its parts, and displays the originality of her world-view and its depiction with a captivating brio. A full and coherent English translation is long overdue.

The translations of the stories were made from the 1978 Slatkine facsimile edition of volume VII of *Le Nouveau Cabinet des Fées*, reproduced on the Bibliothèque Nationale's *gallica* website. The translation of the publisher's prefatory note was made from the copy of volume one of the 1698 edition similarly reproduced on *gallica*.

Brian Stableford

The Publisher To The Reader

Having seen that tales of enchantment have had great success, I requested these, which had been composed some time ago. I was only able to obtain them with difficulty. They have met with such great approval from the persons of quality who have seen them that I am taking no risk in naming them *Les Contes des Contes*.

MORE BEAUTIFUL THAN A FAY

There was once a king in Europe who, having already had several children by a princess that he had married, had a desire to travel and go from one end of his kingdom to the other. He stopped agreeably in various provinces, and when he was in a beautiful castle at the extremity of his states, the queen, his wife, went into labor and gave life to a daughter, who seemed so prodigiously beautiful at the moment of her birth that the courtiers, either because of her beauty or the desire to pay court to her, named her More Beautiful than a Fay. The future made it very evident that she merited such an illustrious name.

The queen was scarcely on her feet again when it was necessary for her to follow the king, her husband, who departed urgently to go and defend a distant province that his enemies were attacking. Little More Beautiful than a Fay was left with her governess and the ladies that were necessary to her. She was raised with a great deal of care, and as her father had to sustain a long and cruel war, she had the leisure to grow and be embellished. Her beauty rendered her famous throughout the surrounding lands; people talked about nothing else. At twelve years old she might have been mistaken for a divinity rather than a mortal person. One of her brothers came to see her during a truce and linked himself with her in a perfect amity.

However, the renown of her beauty and the name that she bore irritated the fays against her to such an extent that they thought about nothing but avenging themselves on her for the pride of her name and destroying a beauty that caused them so much jealousy.

The queen of the fays was not one of those good fays who are the protectors of virtue and who only take pleasure in doing good. After the passage of several centuries, when she had succeeded to her royalty by means of her great knowledge and her artifice, the number of her years had rendered her very small, and no one any longer called her anything but Nabote.[8]

Nabote therefore assembled her council and made it known to its members that she had resolved to avenge the many beautiful persons that she had in her court, and all those who were in the entire world, that she wanted to absent herself and go personally to see and steal the beauty that was causing so much talk disadvantageous to their charms.

Having said it, that was what she did. She departed, and, putting on simple clothes, she transported herself to the castle where the marvel was contained. She soon made herself familiar there, and by means of her intelligence she persuaded the princess's ladies to receive her among them.

Nabote was struck by a great astonishment, however, when she realized, by the force of her art, after having studied the castle, that it had been constructed by a great magician, and that he had attached such virtue to it that people could only emerge voluntarily from its enclosure and its promenades, and it was not possible to make use of charms of any kind against its inhabitants.

That secret was not unknown to More Beautiful than a Fay's governess, who, knowing full well what a

---

[8] i.e., Dwarf.

priceless treasure had been confided to her care, nevertheless loved her without dread, knowing that no one in the world could take the child away as long as she did not leave the castle or its gardens. She had forbidden her expressly to do that, and More Beautiful than a Fay, who already had a good deal of prudence, was careful not to fail in that precaution. A thousand lovers that she had made futile efforts to abduct her, but, living in security, she had no fear of any violence.

It did not take long for Nabote to insinuate herself into her good graces; she taught her to do beautiful needlework; during tasks that she rendered amusing, she told her little stories, and neglected nothing to entertain her. She pleased her so much that soon, neither of them was seen without the other.

In all these cares, Nabote was no less occupied with her vengeance; she was seeking a means to seduce More Beautiful than a Fay and to oblige her, by means of cunning, simply to set foot outside the threshold of the castle; she was always ready to make her move and kidnap her.

One day, when she had taken her into the garden, where young women, after having picked flowers, were ornamenting More Beautiful than a Fay's lovely head, Nabote opened a little door that opened to the countryside, and, having gone through it, she performed a hundred capers that made the princess and the young people with her laugh. Then, suddenly, the wicked Nabote pretended to feel ill, and a moment later she let herself fall, as if she had fainted. A few of the young women ran to help her; More Beautiful than a Fay hastened too.

Scarcely had the unfortunate princess passed through the fatal doorway than Nabote got up again, seized her with a powerful arm and, making a circle with her wand, formed a thick black fog. Although it dissipated immediately, the earth opened up and two moles with wings of rose leaves emerged, drawing an ebony chariot. Nabote got into it with More Beautiful than a Fay, and it rose into the air, traveling with an incredible speed. It was swiftly lost to the sight of the young women, who, by their tears and their screams, soon announced to the entire castle the loss that it had just suffered.

More Beautiful than a Fay only recovered from her initial astonishment to fall into one more frightful; the rapidity with which the chariot flew through the air left her so dazed that she almost lost consciousness. Eventually, recovering her senses, she looked down; how terrified she was to find nothing beneath her but the prodigious extent of a vast sea!

She uttered a piercing scream and turned round. Seeing her dear Nabote close by she embraced her tenderly and clasped her tightly in her arms, as once does customarily to reassure oneself; but the fay pushed her away rudely.

"Get away, brazen child," she said to her. "Recognize in me your most mortal enemy. I am the Queen of the Fays; you are going to pay for the insolence of the name you bear."

More Beautiful than a Fay, more tremulous on hearing those words than if a thunderbolt had landed at her feet, was even more frightened by them than by the horrible route she was taking.

The chariot finally landed in the middle of the magnificent courtyard of the most superb palace that was ever seen.

The sight of such a beautiful place reassured the timid princess slightly, especially when, on emerging from the chariot, she saw a hundred young beauties, who came very courteously to make reverence to the fay. Such a cheerful abode did not seem to announce misfortune. She even had a consolation, which could not fail to be welcome in a misfortune as great as hers; she noticed that all those beautiful persons were struck with admiration as they looked at her, and she heard a confused murmur of praise and envy, which gave her a marvelous satisfaction.

But that moment of vanity did not last long! Nabote ordered imperiously that More Beautiful than a Fay's beautiful clothes should be taken away, believing that that would rob her of a part of her charms. She was therefore stripped, but Nabote's fury only increased in consequence. What beauties came to light! What confusion for Fay society!

She was dressed in wretched rags, but one might have thought that simple and naïve beauty was determined to triumph in that state over the most ostentatious display; she had never been more charming.

Nabote ordered that she be taken to the place that she had organized for her, and given her task.

Two fays took hold of her and escorted her to the most sumptuous and beautiful apartments that could ever be seen. More Beautiful than a Fay considered them; in spite of the sight of her misery she said to herself: *Whatever torments are being prepared for me, my heart tells me that I shall not always be unhappy in this beautiful place.*

She was made to go down a large black marble staircase, which had more than a thousand steps; she thought she was going into the bowels of the earth, or that she was being taken to Hell. Finally, she went into a small cabinet paneled in ebony, where she was told that she would sleep on a little straw, and where there was an ounce of bread and a cup of water for her supper. From there she was taken into a large gallery, the walls of which were made of black marble from top to bottom, and which only received illumination from five lamps made of jet, which emitted a somber glow, more capable of inducing alarm than reassurance. Those sad walls were hung with cobwebs from top to bottom, the fatality of which was such that the more one removed them, the more they multiplied.

The two fays told the princess that the gallery had to be cleaned by daybreak, or else she would be made to suffer frightful tortures. Placing a ladder in her hands and giving her a rush broom, they told her to get to work, and left her to it.

More Beautiful than a Fay sighed, and, not knowing the fate of the cobwebs, even though the gallery was huge, she decided courageously to obey the order. She took her broom and climbed the ladder nimbly. But—Oh God!—imagine her surprise when, thinking that she was clearing the marble and getting rid of the cobwebs, she found that they only increased. She soon wearied, and, seeing sadly that her efforts were futile, she threw away the broom, came down, sat on the bottom step of the ladder and started to weep softly, aware of the extent of her misfortune.

Her sobs had become so precipitate, one after another, that she no longer had the strength to sustain her beautiful body, when, raising her head slightly, her eyes were struck by a bright light. The entire gallery was illuminated in an instant, and she saw a young boy on his knees before her, so handsome, so agreeable and so well-dressed that she mistook him for Amour. But she remembered that Amour was depicted nude, and the handsome boy had a coat covered with gems. She also suspected that all the light might be coming from his eyes, which she saw so beautiful and so brilliant.

The youth considered her, still on his knees, and she wanted to kneel down too.

"Who are you?" she asked him, astonished. "Are you a god? Are you Amour?

"I'm not a god," he replied, "but I have more amour in myself alone than there is in Heaven or on earth. I'm Phraates,[9] the son of the queen of the fays, who loves you and wants to help you."

Then, taking the broom that she had thrown away, he touched all the cobwebs, which immediately became a golden fabric of marvelous workmanship; the glow of the lamps became bright and luminous, and Phraates gave the princess a golden key.

"You'll find a lock," he told her, "in the paneling of your cell; open it very quietly. I'll go, for fear of rendering myself suspect; go and rest, you'll find everything you need. Adieu."

And, putting one knee on the floor, he kissed her hand respectfully.

More Beautiful than a Fay, more astonished by that encounter than by anything that had happened to her during the day, went back into the little room and tried to find the lock that had been mentioned to her.

On approaching the paneling, she heard a voice, the most likeable in the world, which seemed to be lamenting dolorously; she thought that it was an unfortunate

---

[9] Phraates was the name of several kings of ancient Parthia; the name would have been known in the salons of Louis XIV's court because of the publicity given to it there by Jacques Benigne Bossuet's history of the world.

like herself who was being tormented. She listened curiously.

"Alas, what can I do?" said the voice. "They want me to change the acorns in this bushel into Oriental pearls."

More Beautiful than a Fay, less surprised by that than she would have been two hours before, knocked on the wood two or three times and said, quite loudly: "If punishments are inflicted here, miracles are also worked; don't give up hope. But tell me, I beg you, who you are, and I'll tell you who I am."

"It's more pleasant for me to satisfy you, "replied the other, "than to continue my employment. I'm the daughter of a king; it's said that I was born charming; the fays were not present at my birth, and you know that they are cruel to those they don't take under their protection at birth."

"I know that only too well," said More Beautiful than a Fay. "I'm beautiful like you, the daughter of a king, and unfortunate, because I'm lovable without the aid of their gifts."

"We're companions, then?" said the other. "But are you in love?"

"There has scarcely been time," said More Beautiful than a Fay to herself, in a low voice, but she went on, loudly: "Go on, and don't ask me any more questions."

"I was deemed," the other went on, "to be the most charming thing that there had ever been; everyone loved me and wanted to possess me. I was named Desire; all wills were submissive to me and I had a place in all hearts. A young prince, more smitten with me than any other, attached himself uniquely to me; I filled him with hope and satisfaction. We were going to unite ourselves forever when the fays, jealous of seeing me the object of universal passion and unable to tolerate the charms that they had not bestowed, abducted me one day in the midst of my glory and put me here in a vile place. They have told me that they will strangle me tomorrow morning if I haven't carried out a ridiculous order that they've imposed on me. Now tell me who you are."

"I'll have told you everything," replied More Beautiful than a Fay, "when I've told you my name, which is More Beautiful than a Fay."

"You must be very beautiful, then, said Princess Desire. "I have a great desire to see you.

"I have as much desire for my part," replied More Beautiful than a Fay. "Is there a door that opens in this wall, for I have a little key that might be useful to you?"

While searching, she found one, which she was, indeed, able to open. She pushed it, and, suddenly appearing to one another, they were both greatly surprised by the marvelous beauty that they each possessed.

After they had embraced one another fervently, and saying many obliging things, More Beautiful than a Fay started laughing on seeing that Princess Desire was constantly rubbing her acorns with a little white stone, as she had been ordered to do. She told her about the task that she had been given to do, and how a kind unknown force had assisted her miraculously.

"But what can it be?" Princes Desire asked her.

"I believe it's a man," replied More Beautiful than a Fay.

"A man!" cried Desire. "You're blushing; you love him!"

"Not yet," she replied, "but he told me that he loves me, and if he loves me, as he says, he'll help you."

Scarcely had she spoken those words than the bushel shivered, agitating the acorns, as the oak from which they had been collected might have done. They suddenly changed into the most beautiful pear-shaped pearls, of the highest clarity; it was one of them of which Cleopatra made such a rich banquet for Mark Antony.

The two princesses were very content with that change, and More Beautiful than a Fay, who was beginning to get accustomed to prodigies, took Desire by the hand, and drew her into her room. There she found the panel the contained the lock that had been mentioned to her; she opened it with the golden key and went into a room whose magnificence surprised and impressed her, because she saw evidence of the cares of her lover everywhere therein. It was strewn with the most beautiful flowers and exhaled a divine perfume.

At one of the ends of the charming room there was a table covered with everything that could content delicacy of taste, and two fountains of liquors that flowered into porphyry basins. The young princesses sat down in two ivory chairs enriched with emeralds. They ate with appetite, and when they had supped, the table disappeared. In the place where it had been, a delightful bath appeared, into which they both climbed. A few steps away they saw a superb dressing-room containing large hampers with gold hampers, full of linen so clean that it communicated a desire to make use of it.

A bed of singular form and extraordinary richness terminated the marvelous room, which was bordered by orange-trees in golden pots garnished with rubies and cornelian columns that sustained the sumptuous vault all around its perimeter; they were only separated by huge crystal mirrors that extended from the floor to the ceiling. A few small tables in rare materials supported vases of precious stone full of flowers of all kinds.

Princess Desire admired her companion's good fortune. Turning toward her, she said: "You lover is gallant; he can do a great deal, and he wants to do everything for you. Your luck is uncommon."

A pendulum clock chiming midnight caused them to hear the name of Phraates at every stroke. More Beautiful than a Fay blushed, and threw herself on to her bed; she thought she would seek repose, which was troubled by the image of Phraates.

The next day there was a great astonishment in the fay court, on seeing the gallery so richly decorated and the beautiful pearls filing the bushel. They had thought that they would be able to punish the young princesses; their cruelty was disconcerted, and they found each of them withdrawn to her little room.

Agitating their council again to give them further tasks in which they would see them defeated, they told Desire to go to the sea shore and write in the sand, with the express order that what she wrote would never be effaced, and they commanded More Beautiful than a Fay to go to the foot of Mount Adventurous, fly up to the summit and bring them back a vase full the water of immortality. To that effect, they gave her feathers and wax in order for her to make wings and doom herself like another Icarus.

Desire and More Beautiful than a Fay looked at one another after that frightful command, embraced one another tenderly, and separated, as if saying their final adieu. One was escorted to the shore and the other to the foot of Mount Adventurous.

When More Beautiful than a Fay was alone, she took the feathers and the wax and assembled them as best she could. After she had toiled fruitlessly, her thoughts turned to Phraates. "If you love me," she said, "you'll come to my aid again."

Scarcely had she finished the last word than she saw him before her eyes, a thousand times more handsome than the previous night. Broad daylight was very advantageous to him.

"Do you doubt my love?" he said. "Is anything difficult for someone who loves you."

Then he asked her to take off some of her clothes and, having taken his usual recompense, which was a kiss on her hand, he suddenly transformed himself into a eagle. She experienced some chagrin in seeing that lovable figure change in that fashion, but he placed himself at her feet, spreading his wings, and easily made her understand his design. She lowered herself on to him, and put her beautiful arms around his superb neck. He rose gently into the air. One would not have been able to say which of them was the most content: her, in evading death by carrying out the order given to her; or him, in being charged with such a precious burden.

He carried her gently to the top of the mountain, where she heard an agreeable harmony of a thousand birds, which came to render homage to the divine bird that had carried her. The top of the mountain was a florid plain surrounded by beautiful cedars, in the middle of which was a little stream, the silvery waters of which flowed over golden sand strewn with brilliant diamonds. More Beautiful than a Fay knelt down and, before anything else, she put her hand in the precious water and drank some of it. After that she filled her vase and turned to her eagle.

"Oh," she said, "how I wish that Desire had some of this water!"

Scarcely had she said that than the eagle flew down, picked up one of More Beautiful than a Fay's slippers, came back to fill it with water, and went to take it to Princess Desire on the sea shore, where she was employed in writing on that arena, futilely.

The eagle came back to find More Beautiful than a Fay and resume his beautiful burden.

"Alas," she said, what is Desire doing? Bring us together."

He obeyed. They found her still writing, but as she wrote, a wave came to efface what she had written.

"What cruelty," said the princess to More Beautiful than a Fay, "to order me to do what cannot be done. I judge by the strange mount that I see you astride that you've succeeded."

More Beautiful than a Fay got down and, touched by her companion's misfortune, she turned to her lover and said: "Show me you omnipotence."

"Or rather my love," retorted the prince, reverting to his ordinary form.

Desire, seeing the beauty and the grace of his person, made surprise and joy shine in her eyes.

More Beautiful than a Fay blushed, and with an involuntary movement, she placed herself in front of him in order to hide him from her companion. "Do as you're told," she continued, with a charming anxiety.

Phraates, aware of his good fortune, and wanting to terminate her embarrassment, said: "Read," and disappeared more rapidly than a flash of lighting.

At the same moment a wave came to break at More Beautiful than a Fay's feet, and, on retreating, allowed her to see a bronze table mounted in the arena, as if it had been there for all eternity and as if it would still be there until the end of the world. As she looked at it she saw letters that were formed, profoundly engraved, which composed these lines:

The faith of vulgar lovers,
Their ardor and all their oaths,
Are only written in sand,
But what one senses for your lovely eyes
In characters of starlight, is written in the skies;
Whoever tried to erase it would strive in vain.

"I understand," exclaimed Desire. "Whoever loves you must love forever. How well your obliging lover expresses his tenderness!" Then she embraced More Beautiful than a Fay, who, dissipating in her arms the slight jealousy she had just felt, confessed to her friend the conflict that had taken place, and, both satisfied in their amity, they abandoned themselves to an agreeable conversation full of sincerity.

Queen Nabote sent someone to the foot of the mountain to discover what had become of More Beautiful than a Fay. Nothing was found but scattered feathers and some of her clothes; it was judged that she had been crushed, as desired.

Thinking that, the fays hastened to the sea shore. They cried out on seeing the bronze table, and were frightened on seeing the two princesses enjoying themselves tranquilly on a spur of rock. They called out to them; More Beautiful than a Fay gave them her water of immortality and laughed softly, along with Desire, at the fays' fury.

The queen did not see the joke; she knew that an art as great as her own had assisted them, and her rage increased to such a point that, without hesitation, she decided on their complete ruination by the last and most cruel of proofs.

Desire was condemned to go the following day to the Fair of Time, in order to obtain the make-up of youth, and More Beautiful than a Fay to go to the Forest of Marvels, in order to capture the hind with the silver hooves.

Princess Desire was taken to a great plain, on the edge of which was a prodigious building divided into halls and galleries full of boutiques so superb that in order to find a comparison one had to remember the magnificent banks of Marly.[10] In each of those boutiques there were young and agreeable fays, and next to them, to assist them, the persons they loved the most.

As soon as Desire appeared, her beauty charmed everyone; she took possession of all hearts. In the first boutiques she went into, she excited great pity when she asked for the make-up of youth; no one wanted to tell her where it could be fund, because when it was not a fay who came in search of it, a torture was designated for the person charged with that dangerous commission.

The good fays told Desire to turn back and not to ask any longer for what she was seeking. She was so beautiful that everyone ran toward her wherever she went. Her bad luck brought her to the boutique of a malevolent fay. Scarcely had she asked for the make-up of youth on the part of the queen of the fays than, launching a terrible glance at her, she told her that she had it and would give it to her the next day, and ordered her to go

---

[10] There was a so-called *banque* [bank, in the financial sense], associated with retail establishments, in Marly, where Louis XIV's court frequently employed the Château de Marly as a base before the completion of the Palais de Versailles.

into a room to wait while it was being prepared. But she was put into a dark and stinking place where she could not see anything. She was gripped by terror.

"Ah!" she said. "Obliging lover of More Beautiful than a Fay, hasten to help me, or I'm doomed."

He was either deaf to her voice or incapable of acting in that place as he had done in others. Desire was in torment for part of the night, and slept for the rest. She was woken up by a agreeable young woman, who told her, while bringing her a little nourishment, that she had come on behalf of the favorite of the fay who was her mistress, who had resolved to help her; that she would be fortunate if that happened, because the fay had sent for an evil spirit, in order that he might come to blow ugliness into her nose, and that in that deformed and ignominious state she would send her back to the queen of the fays in order to serve for the triumph of her resentments.

Princess Desire thought she would die of fright at the threat of suddenly losing all her charms, and she wished that she might die. Her torment was horrible, she was groping her way around her dark abode when someone took her by the arm and she felt a very tender emotion in her heart. She was taken toward a little light, and when her sight was restored it was struck by the most charming object of all. She recognized the dear prince that loved her so much, from whom she had been separated on the eve of her wedding.

Her transports and joys were extreme. "Is it really you?" she said, a hundred times.

Finally, when she was fully convinced, forgetting all her present misfortunes, she continued: "But is it you who are the favorite of that wretched fay? Is it with that fine title that I see you?"

"Have no doubt about it," he replied, "And we shall owe to her the end of all our troubles and our good fortune."

Then he told her that, in despair at her abduction, he had gone to find a sage, who had told him where she was, and that he would only ever recover her from the realm of the fays; that he had given him the means to find her, but that he had been stopped initially by the cruel fay, who had fallen in love with him; that, following the advice of his sage, he had amused her and, by his tenderness, had rendered himself so much the master of her mind that he retained all her treasures and was the minister of all her desires; that she had just departed on a voyage of six thousand leagues and would not be back for twelve days, so it was necessary to run away; that he had gone to her cabinet to take a fragment of the stone of the ring of Gyges, which she put on in order that she could go anywhere she liked invisibly; that, as for himself, he could show himself freely.

"Don't forget the make-up of youth," she said to him. "I want to put it on and give it to a companion I have."

The prince laughed.

"Where are we going" she asked.

"To the home of the queen of the fays," he said.

"Not that!" she cried. "We'll perish there."

"The sage who advises me," he went on, "told me to take you back to the last place from which you had departed if I wanted to ensure my happiness; he has never lied to me about anything whatsoever."

"All right," said Desire. "Let's go, then."

The prince gave her a precious box that contained the make-up of youth, and in the desire to appear more beautiful in her lover's eyes she rubbed it on her face precipitately, forgetting that she was invisible because of the stone he had given her. She took him by the arm. They traversed the entire fair in that fashion, and went all the way to the queen's palace.

There the prince took back the stone of Gyges. The amiable Desire showed herself and he became invisible, to the great regret of the princess, whose arm he took in his turn, and they went into Nabote's court.

All the fays gazed with a marvelous astonishment on seeing Desire return with the make-up of youth, and the queen frowned.

"Let her be strictly guarded," she said. "Our cleverness is vain; it's necessary to cause her death without going about it in such a roundabout way."

That was the sentence pronounced. Desire trembled with fear on hearing it; her lover reassured her as best he could.

But let us return to More Beautiful than a Fay. She had been taken to the Forest of the Marvelous; and this is why she had been required to hunt the hind with the silver hooves.

There had once been a queen of the fays who had succeeded to that great title naturally; she was beautiful, good and wise; she had had several lovers, whose love and cares were wasted in her regard; uniquely occupied in protecting her virtue, she did not amuse herself listening to the sighs of lovers. There was one of them whom her rigors rendered most unhappy, because he loved her more than any of their others. One day, seeing that he could not bend her, he protested to her in his despair that he would kill himself; she was unmoved by that threat and considered it as one of those follies by which the minds of men are often attained but which do not go any further. However, some time afterwards he threw himself into the sea.

A sage who had brought up the young man complained to the supreme intelligences, and the chaste fay was condemned to be a hind for a hundred years, as a penance for her rigor, unless an accomplished beauty who wanted to risk hunting for ten days in the Forest of Marvels could capture her and return her to her original form. Nearly forty years had already passed since she had been transformed.

In the beginning, several beauties had taken the risk of attempting such a bold adventure, which promised so much glory, each of them believing that they would be the most fortunate; but as none of them had come back, after ten years no more mention was heard of it, the ardor having cooled, and no beauty had been seen to offer herself for a long time, so that those who had been taken there since had only gone by order of the fays, in order to abandon them to certain death.

It was also to get rid of More Beautiful than a Fay that she was taken to the Forest of Marvels. She was given a small provision of food, purely for form's sake, and a silken rope with a noose, with which to catch the hind. That was the whole of her hunting equipment.

She set down what she had been given at the foot of a tree, and when she saw that she was alone she directed her sight into the vast forest, in whose profound silence and solitude she could only see an object of despair.

She wanted to remain on the edge of the forest and not go any deeper into it, and in order to get her bearings she marked the place from which she departed. She was abused, however, one always went astray in that forest, without being able to get out of it.

She perceived the hind with the silver hooves walking gravely along a trail, and went after her with her rope in hand, thinking she could capture her, but the hind ran, sensing that she was pursued, stopping from time to time and turning her head toward More Beautiful than a Fay. They were together all day without getting any closer to one another, and night separated them.

The poor huntress found herself very weary and very hungry, but she did not know where the meager provisions she had been given were, and she could not obtain any repose because of the hard ground. She lay down under a tree, very sadly; she could not sleep for long; she was too scared; the slightest sound frightened her, an agitated leaf making her tremble. She turned over and over in that wretched state, her thoughts directed toward her lover. She appealed to him several times, and, seeing that he was lacking when she was in such great need, she shed a few tears and said to herself: "Oh, Phraates, Phraates, have you abandoned me?"

She was falling asleep when she felt an agitation beneath her, and it seemed to her that she was in the best bed in the world. Her slumber lasted a long time without being interrupted. She was woken up in the morning by the song of a thousand nightingales, and, turning her beautiful eyes, she saw that she was two feet above the ground; the grass had grown under her beautiful body and had acquired the virtue of making a delightful couch. A huge orange tree extended its branches over her to serve as a awning; she was covered with flowers. Alongside her, two turtle-doves announced to her, by means of their love, that she ought to put her hope in Phraates' amour. The ground around her was covered strawberries and all kinds of the most excellent fruits; she ate some, and found herself as sated and as strong as the finest meat would have achieved. A stream that was running nearby served to slake her thirst..

"Oh, cares of my lover," she exclaimed, when she was fully satisfied, "how necessary you were to me. I won't murmur any more, but don't give me so much, and show yourself."

She would have continued if she had not seen the hind with the silver feet, sitting on her hindquarters and gazing at her tranquilly. She thought she had her this time; she presented her with a handful of grass in one hand, and held her rope in the other, but the hind drew away with short bounds, and when she had covered a short distance she stopped and looked at her.

They played that game all day.

Night fell, and she spent it as she had the one before.

The awakening was like the first, and four days and four nights passed in the same fashion.

Finally, on the fifth morning, More Beautiful than a Fay, on opening her eyes, thought that she was seeing a light brighter than daylight when she perceived in her lover's eyes the amour that she had inspired in him. He was sitting beside her and kissing the tip of her foot. His presence and his respectful action pleased him a great deal.

"It's you then?" she said. "If I haven't seen you in recent days, at least I've received marks of your generosity."

"Say my amour, More Beautiful than a Fay," he said. "My mother suspects that it's me who is helping you, and he has me guarded. I escaped briefly, thanks to a friendly fay. Adieu; I only came to reassure you; you'll see me his evening, and if Fortune wishes it, we'll be happy tomorrow."

He went away, and again she hunted all day. When night fell, she perceived a little light nearby, which sufficed for her to look around for her lover.

"Here is my lighted wand," he said. "Hold it in front of you and go, without being frightened, wherever it takes you. When it stops, you'll find a large heap of dry leaves. Set fire to them, go into the place that you see, and if you find the remains of an animal there, burn it. Our friends the heavenly bodies will do the rest."

More Beautiful than a Fay would certainly have liked to receive more ample instructions, but, seeing that there was no remedy, she held the wand in front of her, which showed her the way. She walked for nearly two hours, rather bored with doing nothing but that. She finally stopped, and did, indeed, see a large heap of dry leaves, to which she did not fail to set fire.

The light was soon so bright that she was able to perceive a fairly high mountain, in which she perceived an opening partly hidden by brushwood. She parted it with her wand and went into a dark place. Soon afterwards, she found herself in a large hall ornamented with an admirable architecture and illuminated by several lights. What struck her with some astonishment, however, was seeing the skins of several wild and terrible beasts hanging from golden hooks, which she mistook at first for the beasts themselves. She turned her eyes away with some horror and they paused in the middle of the room, where there was a beautiful palm tree; and on one of the branches was the skin of the hind with the silver hooves.

More Beautiful than a Fay was delighted to see it, and, picking it up with her wand, she immediately took it to the fire that she had lit at the entrance to the lair. It was consumed in an instant. Returning to the hall, she penetrated into several more magnificent rooms. She stopped in one, where she saw several small beds standing on the Persian carpet, one of which was more beautiful than the others, under an awning of gold cloth. But she did not have the leisure to contemplate for long something that seemed so singular to her; she heard loud bursts of laughter and several people talking loudly.

More Beautiful than a Fay turned her steps in that direction. She went into a marvelous place where there were fifteen young women of divine beauty.

She did not surprise them any less than they surprised her; the excellence of her person charmed them all, and caused a suspension of all their senses. An attentive silence was followed by cries of admiration. But one of the beautiful women, more beautiful than all the rest, advanced with a jovial expression, laughing, toward the charming princess.

"You are my liberator," she said to her. I cannot doubt it; no one enters here who has not put on the skin of one of the animals that you have seen at the entrance to this cavern; that has been the fate of all these beautiful persons you see beside me. After ten days of fruitless attempts to capture me, they were changed into animals during the day, and by night we recover our human faces. And if you had not liberated me, charming princess, you would have been changed into a white rabbit."

"A white rabbit!" cried More Beautiful than a Fay. "Oh, Madame, it's much better that I have conserved my ordinary form, and that such a marvelous person as you is no longer a hind."

"You have set all of us free," said the fay. "Let's spend the rest of the night joyfully, and tomorrow we shall go to the palace and fill the entire court with astonishment."

It is impossible to describe the delight that resounded in that charming dwelling and the excitement of all those beautiful young women who were about to enjoy the sweetness of living again, so to speak. They were all the same age at which they had commenced their hunt in the Forest of Marvels, and the oldest of them was not twenty years old.

The fay wanted to go to bed for three or four hours; she had More Beautiful than a Fay go to bed with her, and desired to know her adventure. She related it to her in such a touching fashion, her speech was so simple and truthful that the fay promised without reserve to serve her amour and render her happy. More Beautiful than a Fay did not forget to speak to her about Desire, and the fay was immediately favorable to her.

They went to sleep after a rather long conversation, which they interrupted agreeably with the charming caresses that they gave one another.[11]

The following day they all took the road to the palace, wanting to surprise the fays agreeably. They quit the Forest of Marvels without regret, and arrived at the palace quietly. When they were near the final courtyard they heard a thousand harmonious voices, which composed an excellent music.

---

[11] In considering the significance of this assertion, and this entire passage, it might be worth recalling that neither Mademoiselle de La Force nor Mademoiselle de L'Héritier ever married, that Mademoiselle de Scudéry always preferred to be known by the nickname "Sapho" and that one of the charges laid against the Comtesse de Murat in a report drawn up by the Lieutenant of Police before she was banished from the court was that of indulging in lesbian practices. How much light that might cast on the origins of *contes de fées*, and hence of modern fantasy fiction, is a matter of pure conjecture.

"It's some kind of celebration," said the fay. "We've arrived at a good time."

And, on advancing, they found the courtyard filled with an incredible crowd.

They fay had the door opened and passed through it with her troop. The first to recognize her uttered cries to the heavens, and they were soon the subject of a great joy; but as they advanced further she was struck by a strange spectacle. She saw a young woman, more charming than the Graces and as fair as Venus, who was attached to a stake next to a pyre, where she was apparently about to be burned.

More Beautiful than a Fay uttered a loud scream, recognizing Desire, but she was very surprised when, at the same moment, she could no longer see her, and a young man appeared in her stead, so beautiful and so well-built that one could not weary of looking at him.

At that sight, More Beautiful than a Fay uttered a much louder scream, and, running without any further restraint, she threw her arms around him, crying a thousand times: "It's my brother!"

It was her brother, who was also the fortunate lover of Princess Desire, and who, fearing that she might die, had just given her the ring of Gyges in order to shield her from the cruelty of Queen Nabote. By that means, he had revealed himself.

While the brother and sister were giving one another that evidence of tenderness, the invisible Desire mingled hers with them, and her voice made itself heard although her body did not appear. All the fays, in an unparalleled astonishment, gave striking evidence in a thousand different fashions of their joy at seeing their virtuous queen again. The good fays came to throw themselves at her feet, kissing her hands and her garments.

They wept, they lost the power of speech; each one expressed herself in accordance with her character. The bad fays, the partisans of Nabote, also hastened around her, and politics gave an air of sincerity to their false demonstrations.

Nabote herself, in despair at that return, constrained herself with an art of which she alone was capable. She was obliged to yield her power immediately to the veritable queen, who, in a grave and majestic manner, asked why the young woman she had seen merited such a torture, and since when had such a cruel death been solemnized by feasting and games. Nabote excused herself very poorly, and the queen was listening impatiently when Desire's lover spoke out.

"That princess was being punished," he said, "because she was too lovable. The princess my sister was tormented for the same reason. They were both born as you see them." Then he asked his mistress to take off the stone of Gyges, and she became visible. Having reappeared, Desire charmed everyone who saw her.

"They're beautiful," the prince went on, "they have a thousand virtues that they did not obtain from the fays; that is what has roused them and obliged them to persecute them. What injustice, to want to extend tyrannical power over everything that does not depend on you!"

The prince fell silent. The queen turned to the assembly with an agreeable expression. "I demand," she said, "that these three persons are given to me; they shall have the happiest of fates that mortals can have. I owe a great deal to More Beautiful than a Fay and I shall recompense her for what she has done for me with the most constant happiness."

Turning toward Nabote, she continued: "You shall reign, Madame; this empire is large enough for you and me. Go to the beautiful isles, which will belong to you. Leave me your son; I shall associate him with my power and I want him to marry More Beautiful than a Fay; that union will reconcile us all."

Nabote was enraged by everything the queen ordered, but what could she do? She was not the stronger; she had no alternative but to obey. She was about to do so with an ill grace when the handsome Phraates was seen arriving, followed by a gallant company of youths which composed his court; her came to render his homages to the queen and to rejoice in her return. In passing however he glanced at More Beautiful than a Fay and enabled her to see, by his passionate gaze, that it was only his first duty,

The queen embraced him and introduced More Beautiful than a Fay to him, asking him to receive her hand. It was unnecessary to ask him whether he obeyed with joy, as he cried with delight:

> God of lovers you repay the confidence
> Of a thousand amorous labors;
> You will become, to fulfill all my wishes,
> My pleasure and my recompense.

The two marriages were celebrated on the same day; they were so happy that it was said that they were the only spouses who earned the golden vine, and that those of whom there has been mention since have only had the idea of it.

Thus, virtue triumphs over the misfortunes it provokes. Envy and jealousy only serve to make it shine, and the justice of heaven often permit it to be happy.

There is a destiny that watches over the conduct of humans, and enables them to overcome everything that tries to oppose her happiness.

> *Born under a prosperous star,*
> *Without being fashioned by art;*
> *Everything will succeed for you, the cruelest affair*
> *Will be rendered good one day by a stroke of luck.*
> *Fortune overwhelms us for a while,*
> *But only to assist us better;*
> *Happiness makes itself taste better*
> *To those who remember a wretched state.*
> *A wicked fay displays her power,*
> *Always raising obstacles to virtue,*
> *In these times fays are no longer seen*
> *But one no longer sees miracles.*
> *

PERSINETTE

Two young lovers were married after a long pursuit of their amour; nothing equaled their ardor; they were living content and happy when, to complete their felicity, the young wife found that she was pregnant, and there was a great joy in the little household; they had wanted a child so much, and their desire had been accomplished.

In their vicinity there was a fay who was curious, above all, for having a beautiful garden; one could see therein an abundance of all sorts of fruits, plants and flowers.

In those days, parsley was very rare in these regions; the fay had had some brought from India, and in all the country it was only found in her garden. The new wife had a great desire to eat some, and although she knew very well that it was not easy to satisfy, because nobody went into that garden, she fell into a chagrin that rendered her unrecognizable in her husband's eyes.

He tormented himself trying to find the cause of the prodigious change that appeared in her mind as well as her body, and after having resisted him for a long time, the wife finally confessed that she had a fervent craving to eat parsley. The husband sighed, and was troubled by a desire so difficult to satisfy; nevertheless, as nothing appears to be out of reach in amour, he went around the walls of the garden day and night in order to try and climb into it; but they were so high that they rendered the task impossible.

Finally, he perceived one of the doors to the garden open; he slipped through it, and was so glad that he took a handful of parsley in haste. He got out as he had got in, and took his stolen goods to his wife, who ate it avidly, and who found herself, two days later, more fervent than ever in her desire to eat it again.

Parsley must have tasted very good in those days.

The poor husband went back several times, in vain. Finally, however, his persistence was recompensed; again he found the door to the garden open. He went in, and was very surprised to see the fay herself, who scolded him loudly for his boldness in coming into a place to which entry was not permitted to anyone at all.

The confused young man got down on his knees and asked her for a gift, saying that his wife might die if she did not eat a little parsley; that she was pregnant and that the desire was very forgivable.

"Well," the fay said to him, "I'll give you as much parsley as you wish if you will give me the child to which your wife gives birth."

After a short deliberation, the husband promised that, and he took as much parsley as he wished.

"When the term of the pregnancy arrived, the fay went to the wife, who gave birth to a daughter, to whom the fay gave the name Persinette;[12] she received her in golden swaddling clothes, and washed her face with a precious water that she had in a crystal vase, which immediately rendered her the most beautiful creature in the world.

---

[12] The French word for parsley is *persil*; a case could be made for altering the child's name to "Parslinette" in an English translation, but the original sounds better.

After these ceremonies of beauty, the fay took little Persinette home with her, and had her brought up with all imaginable cares. She was a marvel before she had reached her twelfth year, and as the fay knew her fatality she resolved to shield her from her destiny.[13]

To that effect, by means of her enchantments, she built a silver tower in the middle of a forest. That mysterious tower had no door by which to enter it. It had large and beautiful apartments, so illuminated that if the sunlight entered them, they received light from the fire of the gems with which they were all brilliant. All that was necessary to life as found here splendidly; all rarities were amassed in the place. Persinette had only to open the drawers of her cabinets and she found them full of the most beautiful jewels; her wardrobes were as magnificent as those of the queens of Asia and there was no new fashion that she was not the first to have. She was alone in that beautiful abode, where she had nothing to desire but company; with that exception, all her desires were anticipated and satisfied.

Needless to say, the most delicate dishes formed her nourishment at all her meals. I assure you, however, that as she only knew the fay, she was not bored in her solitude; she read, she painted, she played musical instruments and she amused herself with all the things of which a well brought-up young woman cannot be ignorant.

---

[13] In Basile's story it is an ogress who bargains for possession of the child, and in most later versions that heroine's captor is simply malevolent; La Force's modification of the relationship might be significant in the story's interpretation, and the significance of the tower, here made of silver.

The fay ordered her to sleep at the top of the tower, where there was only a single widow, and after having established her in that charming solitude, she descended via that widow and returned to her home.

As soon as she was alone, Persinette diverted herself with a hundred different things. When she only had to rummage in her boxes, that was a great enough occupation; how many people would like to have a similar one?

The view from the window of the tower was the most beautiful in the world, for the sea could be seen in one direction and in the other the vast forest; those two objects were singular and charming. Persinette had a divine voice and she took great pleasure in singing; that was often her amusement, especially at the times when she was expecting the fay. The fay often came to see her, and when she was at the foot of the tower she was accustomed to say: "Persinette, let down your hair so I can climb up."

Persinette's hair was one of her great beauties; it was thirty aunes long,[14] without inconveniencing her. It was blonde, like fine gold, organized with ribbons of all colors; when she heard the fay's voice she unfastened it and lowered it, and the fay climbed up.

One day, when Persinette was alone at the window she started singing, as prettily as could be. A young prince as hunting at the time; he had gone astray while chasing a stag; on hearing such an agreeable song he drew nearer, and saw young Persinette; her beauty touched him, her voice charmed him. He circled the fatal

---

[14] A French aune was roughly equivalent to the ancient cubit, the distance from the fingertips to the elbow of a man's arm, about eighteen inches.

tower twenty times, and, not seeing any entrance, he thought he might die of dolor; he was in love. He was audacious, and he would have liked to be able to scale the tower.

For her part, Persinette lost the power of speech when she saw such a handsome man; she considered him for a long time in utter astonishment, but she suddenly stepped back from the window, believing that he was some monster, remembering having heard tell that there were some that could kill by means of the eyes, and she had found the gaze of this one very dangerous.

The prince was in despair at seeing her disappear thus; he made enquiries at the nearest habitations as to who she was, and was told that a fay had built the tower and had imprisoned a young woman in it. He prowled around it every day; eventually, he saw the fay arrive and heard what she said: "Persinette, let down your hair so I can climb up." At the same time, he observed that the young woman unfastened the long tresses of her hair and that the fay climbed up them. He was very surprised by such an extraordinary manner of rendering a visit.

The next day when he thought that the hour had passed at which the fay was accustomed to enter the tower, he waited for nightfall with much impatience. Approaching the tower beneath the window he imitated the fay's voice admirably and said: "Persinette, let down your hair so I can climb up."

Poor Persinette, deceived by the sound of that voice, ran to the window and unfastened her beautiful hair. The prince climbed up it, and when he reached the top, able to see through the window, he thought he was about to fall down again when he saw that prodigious beauty at such close range. Recalling all his natural audacity, however, he leapt into the room. Falling at

Persinette's feet, he embraced her knees with a persuasive ardor.

She was frightened at first; she screamed; a moment later she trembled, and nothing was capable of reassuring her until she sensed in her heart as much amour as she had put into that of the prince.

He said the most beautiful things in the world to her, to which she only responded with a disturbance that gave the prince hope. Finally, having become bolder, he proposed to espouse her immediately; she consented to that almost without knowing what she was doing; nevertheless she completed the whole ceremony.

Now that the prince was happy Persinette also became accustomed to loving him; they saw one another every day, and a short time afterwards she found that she was pregnant. That unknown state made her very anxious; the prince suspected as much, and did not want to explain it to her for fear of afflicting her.

The fay having come to see her, however, she had no sooner looked at her than she knew what was wrong with her.

"Wretch," she said, "you have fallen into a great fault. You will be punished for it, destiny cannot be avoided, and my prevision has been in vain."

After saying that she demanded in an imperious tone a full confession of the adventure, which poor Persinette made, her eyes wet with tears.

After hearing that story, the fay did not appear touched by all the love about which Persinette told her in such touching terms, and, taking her by the hair, she cut its precious strands. After that she made her descend, and descended herself, through the window. When they reached the ground she enveloped herself with her in a cloud, which carried them both to the edge of the sea, to a very solitary but quite agreeable place. There were meadows and woods there, a stream of fresh water, and a little hut made of foliage that was still green. There was a bed of marine rushes inside, and a basket alongside it in which were certain biscuits that were rather good, and which never ran out. It was into that place that the fay took Persinette and left her, after having made her reproaches that appeared to her to be a hundred times more cruel than her own woes.

It was in that place that she gave birth to a little prince and a little princess, and it was in the same place that she nourished them, and had plenty of time to bemoan her misfortune.

But the fay did not find that vengeance sufficiently full; it was necessary that she should have the prince in her power and that she punish him too. As soon as she had quit the unhappy Persinette she went back up into the tower and started to sing in the tone in which Persinette sang.

The prince, deceived by that voice when he came back to see her, asked for her hair again in order to climb up, as he was accustomed to do. The perfidious fay had cut off the beautiful Persinette's tresses for that express purpose, and extended them to him. The poor prince climbed up to the window, where he had much less astonishment than dolor in not finding his mistress. He searched for her with his eyes, but the fay looked at him wrathfully.

"Temeritous fellow," she said to him, "Your crime is infinite; its punishment will be terrible."

Without paying any heed to the threats, however, which only regarded him, he responded: "Where is Persinette?"

"She is no longer for you," she replied.

When the prince, more agitated by the fury of his dolor than constrained by the power of the fay's art, threw himself from the top of the tower to the bottom, he should have broken every bone in his body, but he fell without doing himself any other harm than losing his sight.

He was very astonished to find that he could no longer see. He remained at the foot of the tower for some time, moaning and pronouncing Persinette's name a hundred times over.

He walked as best he could, groping at first, but his steps eventually became more assured. He went thus for I know not how long without encountering anyone who was able to assist and guide him. He nourished himself on herbs and roots that he found when hunger became pressing.

After a few years he found himself, one day, more afflicted by the memory of his amour and his misfortunes than usual. He lay down under a tree and devoted all his thoughts to the sad reflections he was making. That occupation is cruel for someone who thinks he merits a better fate; but suddenly, he was extracted from his reverie by the sound of a charming voice that he heard.

The first sounds went all the way to his heart; thy penetrated it and imported sweet emotions into it that he had had a long time ago but of which he no longer had the habit.

"O gods!" he cried. "That's Persinette's voice!"

He was not mistaken; he had arrived unwittingly in her desert. She was sitting on the doorstep of her cabin and singing the unfortunate story of her amour. Two children that she had, more beautiful than the day, were playing nearby, and, drawing away a little, they arrived at the tree under which the prince was lying. They had no sooner seen him than both of them threw their arms around his neck, kissed him a thousand times and saying continually: "It's my father."

They called their mother, and uttered such cries that she came running, not knowing what it could be; until that moment her solitude had never been troubled by any accident.

What was her surprise and her joy when she recognized her dead husband? It is not possible to describe it. She uttered a piercing scream at the sight of him; the shock was so sensible that, by a perfectly natural effort, she shed a torrent of tears—but, O marvel!—scarcely had her precious tears fallen upon the prince's eyes than they immediately recovered all their light; he could see as clearly as he had before, and he received that favor by virtue of the tenderness of the passionate Persinette, whom he took in his arms and to whom he gave a thousand times more caresses than he had ever done before.

It was a very touching spectacle to see that handsome prince, that charming princess and those lovable children in a joy and tenderness that transported them outside themselves.

The rest of the day went by in that pleasure, but when dusk fell the little family had need of a little nourishment. As the prince thought he was taking some of the biscuit, it was suddenly converted into stone. He was frightened by that prodigy, and sighed with dolor. The poor children wept. The desolate mother wanted at least to give them a little water, but it was changed into crystal.

What a night! They spent it rather poorly; they thought a hundred times that it would be eternal for them.

As soon as daylight appeared, they got up and decided to go and collect a few herbs; but they were transformed into toads and venomous beasts. The most innocent birds became dragons and harpies that flew around them, the sight of which caused terror.

"It's all over, then, my dear Persinette," cried the prince. "I've only found you again in order to lose you in a more terrible fashion."

"Let us die, my dear prince," she replied, kissing him tenderly, "and let us make our enemies envy even the sweetness of our death."

The poor little children were in their arms, in a faint that put them within an inch of death. Who would not have been touched by seeing that deplorable family dying in that fashion? So, a favorable miracle was made for them. The fay was softened, and, recalling at that moment all the tenderness that she had once had for the lovable Persinette, she transported herself to the place where they were. She appeared in a chariot shining with gold and gems; she had them climb into it, placing herself between those fortunate lovers and, putting their lovely children at their feet on magnificent tiles, she took them in that fashion all the way to the palace of the king, the prince's father.

It was there that the delight was excessive; the handsome prince, who had been thought lost for such a long time, was received like a god. He was so satisfied to find himself in repose, after being agitated so stormily, that nothing in the world was comparable to the felicity in which he lived with his perfect wife.

Tender spouses, learn from this
That it is advantageous always to be faithful
Difficulties, labors, the most painful cares,

All are eventually softened
When ardors are mutual;
One braves fortune, one overcomes fate,
As long as two spouses are in accord.

THE ENCHANTER[15]

There was once a king who was called the good king because he was virtuous and just, loved by his subjects and cherished by his neighbors.

As his renown spread throughout the world, another king came into his estates to ask him for a wife. The good king, honored by such confidence, chose the most charming of all his nieces and promised her to him; she was known as Isene the Beautiful.

Such an illustrious marriage was made known throughout the world, in order that everyone might celebrate it with feasts and games; so many people came that it was a marvel.

---

[15] Author's note: "'The Enchanter' is taken from an ancient Gothic book named *Perceval*. Many things have been cut out of it that are not in accordance with our mores. Many others have also been added. A few names have been changed. It is the only tale that is not entirely the author's; all the others are purely of her invention." The note is odd, not least in claiming that "Persinette" is entirely the author's own. The original of the story of Perceval is the fragmentary and enigmatic *Conte du graal* by Chrétien de Troyes, which was published posthumously in juxtaposition with another unfinished romance, *Gawain*, which some commentators mistakenly thought to be its continuation. The hero of that romance was borrowed by the unknown author of the English Medieval romance *Gawain and the Green Knight*, and it is the latter whose striking but deeply enigmatic central motif is appropriated by Mademoiselle de La Force for the present story.

Among so many princes, the Lord of the Distant Isles was extremely noticeable; he was well made and a great enchanter. As soon as he saw Isene the Beautiful he fell in love with her and was very annoyed to see that she was about to be given to another; he flattered himself that if he had arrived sooner, and had asked the good king for her, he would have obtained her.

In that thought, he was afflicted, and tormented his mind regarding the expedients he could employ in order to have the possession of such an accomplished beauty.

The marriage eventually took place, to his great regret, but he made such clever use of his art that on the wedding night, when the bride was put to bed and left alone, in accordance with the custom of the times, she was unable to remain in her bed, by virtue of a secret power. She got up and went into her dressing-room, which was beside her bedroom. She sat down on a little bed, amusing herself looking at the rarities of that beautiful place, that dressing-room being brightly illuminated; but she soon had another occupation when she saw the Lord of the Distant Isles come in.

He knelt down before her and told her that he loved her, and she felt such a great inclination for him that all the magic could not have formed anything similar if it had not been caught up in a natural sentiment.

He said the most beautiful things in the world to the queen; she responded so well that he thought himself fortunate, and confessed that he had put a slave in the king's bed, which he mistook for her. Isene laughed, and spent the night making mock of her husband; and when day came, she appeared as if nothing had happened.

The king, charmed by the good fortune he had had, found himself the most contented of all men, but the Enchanter was the more amorous and the more satisfied.

He carried off all the prizes in the tournaments and he gave a hundred marks of amour to Isene the Beautiful, to which no one paid any heed; they looked at one another surreptitiously; they danced together; they held hands; at table they rank from the same glass. Nothing is comparable to the felicity of the commencements of amour.

On the second night, the Enchanter was with the queen again, and he put his slave in the king's bed. The day passed in those testimonies of amour which, although given mysteriously, have an infinite charm for delicate souls.

The third night was similar to the previous two, so the Enchanter had the same pleasures, which the king also thought he had, in the company of the woman that had been set beside him.

The celebrations having ended, everyone withdrew; the king took his leave of the good king, and took his new wife to his own estates. A short time afterwards she perceived that she was pregnant; and, the term having some, she gave birth to the handsomest prince that was ever seen. He was named Carados.[16]

The king loved him passionately, because he believed himself to be his father, and he queen cherished him with a great tenderness.

He grew visibly, and became more handsome by the day; when he was twelve years old one might have thought that he was eighteen. As soon as he was shown something, he knew it from then on better than his masters. He danced well, sang similarly, rode a horse well,

---

[16] Carados is frequently names in French Arthurian romances as a knight of the round table, like Gawain, and has a central role the first and best known of several continuations of Chrétien de Troyes's *Conte du graal/Gawain*.

carried out all his exercises to perfection, knew history, and was not ignorant of anything that a great prince ought to know.

He heard mention so frequently of the court of the good king that the desire took him to go there. He expressed that desire he king and queen, who criticized him, unable to consent to seeing such a lovable child go away. But young Carados could not suffer the resistance that they put up, and he fell ill with chagrin. Seeing that he was getting worse every day, his father and other decided to satisfy him. They gave him a fine carriage, and after having embraced him a thousand times, they allowed him to depart.

I shall not say how he was received at the court of the good king; that must be obvious. He was given a hundred caresses, and everyone was astonished to see him so well made, handsome and charming.

He completed his perfections in that court; he made war, and performed deeds so fine that there was no talk of anything but his valor.

He was eighteen years old when the king's birthday arrived, which he was accustomed to celebrate with great splendor. He held a plenary court, and ordinarily granted everything that was asked of him. His throne was elevated in a prodigiously large hall, the front of which, overlooking open country, was formed by a great arcade that extended from the top to the bottom, so that those who were coming could easily be seen. It was there that a fine assembly surrounded the king's throne. He had a very beautiful wife, who was beside him, with a large number of princesses and ladies.

There was no thought of anything but rejoicing, and all minds were disposed to pleasure. Carados was shining in that assembly like the rose above other flowers when a cavalier mounted on a fine white horse with an isabelline mane was perceived in the plain, who was advancing with all the grace in the world.

When he was close enough to be discerned it was remarked that he was dressed in green, circled by a magnificent sash, from which a sword hung so brilliant with gems that its glare could not be sustained. The young man was divinely handsome; a hundred curls of blond hair covered his shoulders; he had a crown of flowers on his head, his face was animated by a lively and cheerful expression, and he was singing very agreeable as he went along.

When he was near the hall, he descended lightly to the ground, and the good king's servants well trained, took his horse away and took care of it.

He came into the place where the good king was in such an agreeable fashion that he attracted the gazes of the entire assembly; the ladies, especially, found him charming. He advanced toward the good king's throne with a noble boldness, after having saluted such an illustrious company.

He knelt down before the king, detached his word and laid it at his feet. "Sire," he said, "I have come to ask your majesty for a gift; I hope that his generosity will not refuse it to me on such a solemn day."

"Speak, agreeable stranger," replied the good king. "I do not refuse anything on a day like this, and it is not with you that I shall commence a refusal that is not usual to me. I give you my word that whatever you request, you will obtain."

"That being so, Sire," replied the young man, "I ask you for an *accollée* for an *accollée*."[17]

"What does that mean?" cried the king, very surprised. "You're proposing an enigma instead of asking for a favor; I don't understand you." And when the good king had turned to the assembly, and asked if they knew what the words meant, and had received the response that no one knew what they signified he asked the young man to explain himself better.

"An *accollée* for an *accollée*," the young man replied, "merely means, Sire, except that it is necessary for someone in this assembly to cut off my head with my sword, which is here."

At that request, the assembly uttered a long exclamation of astonishment; the king thought that he was about to fall off his throne in surprise; the queen furrowed her brows in horror, and all the beautiful ladies who were there gave evidence of chagrin.

The good king wanted to excuse himself from keeping such a barbaric promise, and said that he had been taken by surprise; but the young man was obstinate in holding firm, and told the king hat his honor was engaged. The king was as plaintive as possible; he asked whether anyone wanted to carry out that horrible execu-

---

[17] *Accollée*, at the time when the story was written, was one of the many terms conventionally deployed in heraldry to describe the design of an escutcheon. It refers to motifs placed to either side of another, although its literal significance can be construed as "around the neck." The same etymological root thus gave rise to the modern verb *accoler*, to hug, and also to "accolade," a tokenistic kiss on both cheeks. The good king's confusion as to what the stranger means is understandable, but the story's readers would have been aware of all the relevant *double entendres*.

tion, but no one said a word, by which the king was even more annoyed. In vain he testified to the young man that he had just troubled the day's joy cruelly; he remained inflexible in wanting someone to cut off his head.

Finally, Carados came forward and told the king that he was too devoted to him to suffer the insult that the young man wanted to make him by virtue of the impossibility that he believed he had put him of keeping the promise he had made him, and that he was ready to disengage his word.

The young man smiled agreeably as he looked at Carados, and told him that he was ready to receive death. A block was brought; Carados picked up the fatal sword; the young man knelt down; and all eyes were attentive to such an astonishing spectacle when Carados separated the head from the body, which spun three times and bounced three times and then went to replant itself on its trunk; and the young man rose to his feet with a very cheerful disposition.

If everyone had been surprised by the request he had made, they were even more so by his resurrection. After great cries, a silent admiration held sway for a long time over all those seemingly-enchanted minds.

The good king was very pleased by the adventure, and young Carados was even more so, in not having committed an innocent murder; but the young man approached the king cheerfully and knelt down again.

"Sire," he said to him, "I summon you to keep the promise that you have made to me."

"What?" said the king. "Have I not done so?"

"No Sire," he continued, "only half of it. I asked for an *accollée* for an *accollée*. Carados has given one to me; it is now necessary that I return it, and that I cut off his head too."

At that, proposition, every voice was raised, and above all, a thousand feminine cried were heard, which seemed to oppose such a barbaric demand. The king was consternated, the queen and all the ladies bewildered, and the assembly troubled, so much was Carados beloved; only he seemed tranquil, and said to the king that he was only too glad to shed his blood in order to disengage his honor.

The young man was still looking at him, smiling. Turning to the good king, he said: "Sire, I have troubled the pleasure of this celebration enough; this would be too much agitation for one day; I shall postpone the execution to this affair for a year from today, and I beg all these princes and lords to be there. I shall come back on the day in question, for the execution of your promise, and we shall see whether Carados will have sufficient courage to suffer the death that he had the firmness to give me."

After that, they went to table; the banquet was very melancholy, all the guests being saddened by the destiny of Carados.

The year went by in occasions of glory for the prince; he performed a hundred fine deeds and he was the first to return to the hall of the assembly at the end of the year. Everyone was consternated, and their sight was incessantly attached to the direction of the open country, still hoping that perhaps they would not see the man whose arrival they dreaded so much.

He finally appeared, mounted on the same horse, with his green attire, his sash, his beautiful sword and his crown of roses. He was singing, as before, and he came in the same way to the king's feet to request the accomplishment of his promise. The god king begged him in vain to release him from it, and the queen, seeing that the king was not gaining any purchase on his spirit, came with all the ladies to implore him to let Carados live, offering him the most beautiful of the king's nieces, with half the kingdom; but the queen's pleas and tears obtained nothing.

Only Carados did not seem to be moved by the peril that threatened him; he advanced toward the good king with an assured countenance and begged him to finish promptly something that was quite inevitable.

The block was brought forth, and the prince extended his neck. The young man raised his sword and held it in the air for such a long time that Carados, darting glances at him that would have softened the heart of cruelty personified, said to him: "Finish it; you're giving me a thousand deaths for one."

At those words the young man raised is arm further, and then tranquilly returned the sword to its sheath and held out his hand to Carados to lift him up.

"Get up, young prince," he said. "You have given marks of your courage on a hundred occasions; I am very glad that your firmness has been seen."

A thousand cries of joy rose up to the heavens, for such an unexpected success. The good king descended from his throne and came to embrace the young man; the queen, the ladies and the entire assembly resembled troubled individuals rather than rational ones.

The feast was filled with delight, and the young man asked to speak to Carados in private. They both went into a gallery, where the young man, after having given Carados many caresses, told him that he was the Lord of the Distant Isles, and that he was his father.

At that news the prince blushed and his face lit up with anger. He told the Enchanter that that was not true, that he was blackening the reputation of Isene the Beautiful, and that the king, her husband, was his father.

The Enchanter was surprised to receive such an ill-natured response. "You're an ingrate," he said, "but you're nonetheless my son. It's me who endowed you with so many fine qualities, which have made you beloved by everyone. Oh, Carados, I'm afraid that you might repent of the harshness you're testifying to me."

They separated, and a few days later, Carados, who had not believed that he was the Enchanter's son, had a desire to go and see the man whom he believed to be his father. He took his leave of the good king and the queen, and went to find the husband of Isene the Beautiful.

He was received with great demonstrations of amity by the king and the queen, and when he was alone with the king, who spoke to him about the dread that he had had for his death, which an unknown man sought, Carados was imprudent enough to tell him everything that the Enchanter had said to him.

The king, who loved Carados with an infinite tenderness, was struck by his story, and assured him that whatever happened, he would not love him any less, that he would always regard him as his son and his successor, and that he would not have any other, but that it was necessary to clarify the matter with the queen, who might well have had some gallantry with the Lord of the Distant Isles.

They sent for Isene the Beautiful, who fainted on hearing the truth spoken, and appeared only too convinced of it; she did not indulge herself by denying it, but her greatest dolor as to see herself accused and convinced by her own son.

The king consulted Carados as to what remedy might be sought for such a great evil. Carados said that, although the king's shame had been secret, a striking vengeance was required; that it was therefore necessary that the king send for workmen from all parts and employ all his treasures in having a tower of impregnable strength constructed, and that the queen should be imprisoned within it, with a good and reliable guard.

That advice pleased the king and it was executed; in a matter of days the tower was built and the queen was imprisoned within it.

After that, Carados, who felt no remorse at the treatment to which he had subjected his mother, departed in order to return to the court of the good king.

He was no more than two days away from the capital city of his realm, when he perceived something bright in the distance, in a meadow. On coming closer he saw that they were tents, over the largest of which there was a golden ball bearing a great eagle of the same substance, which seemed to be rising into the sky.

Carados advanced toward those tents; he did not see anyone around them. He descended from his horse and went into the one that appeared to be the finest. There was a beautiful bed inside, the curtains of which were raised, and on the bed was a young woman of unparalleled beauty, who was asleep.

The prince was immediately charmed by the sight of such a beautiful object. The first moment was given to admiration, and the second to amour. He was in love without being able to help himself, and, contrary to the custom of grand passions, he was bold, as people are nowadays; he was as bold as he was amorous.

He began by kneeling down, and taking one of the young woman's hands, which he kissed; but his audacity increased. She woke up and was frightened to find herself in the arms of man, whom she did not look at to begin with. She therefore cried out, and was trying to leap out of bed when a Greek slave emerged from a cabinet and came running. At first she extended her arms to her mistress in order to help her, but, casting her eyes upon Carados, she abandoned herself to a great surprise.

"Look at the man you're fleeing," she said to her young mistress, who turned her head toward the prince with wild eyes. They suddenly softened, however, afterwards smiling in an agreeable manner.

"It's Carados," she said, with a great deal of joy. "It's Carados."

"I am undoubtedly Carados," relied the prince, charmed by her tenderness, "but how do you know me?"

"Wait a moment," she said, and, after running into a nearby pavilion with her slave she returned continently holding a large scroll, which she deployed and showed Carados his portrait.

"This is your portrait," she said to him. "As soon as I saw it, I loved you, and as soon as I loved you, I destined myself for you and I obtained a promise from my brother that I would never have any other husband. We are on our way to the court of the good king, where he is going to ask for a wife and to ask for you for my husband. My brother is King Candor, and my name is Adelis."

As she finished speaking, King Candor, who was almost as beautiful as his sister, came into the tent. Adelis introduced Carados to him; from then on they loved one another like brothers, and they went to the court of the good king together.

Everyone there was charmed by the fine manners and beauty of the brother and the sister; the good king introduced all his nieces to King Candor; he chose the most lovable, whom he married.

The marriage of Carados and Adelis was about to be celebrated when a messenger arrived on the part of the king whom he believed to be his father, summoning him with all diligence. He departed, leaving the beautiful Adelis, and promising a prompt return; but is it not the case that things that depend on destiny are not in our power?

When Carados arrived, the king told him that he was in a strange difficulty; that every night, charming melodies were heard in Isene the Beautiful's tower, and that apparently, the Enchanter was taking the trouble to amuse her in her captivity.

He was not mistaken; the Lord of the Distant Isles had been in despair at what the queen had been made to suffer for love of him, and wanted to reduce its rigor by continual testimonies of amour. He had obtained twelve beautiful women, which he had placed next to her, and well made men, who composed an agreeable court, along with the best musicians there were in those days, good dancers and excellent actors. She had comedy three times a week, opera the other nights, and very agreeable celebrations with splendid feasts. He thus helped the time pass that had been intended to cause the queen so much ennui, and he accompanied all those pleasures with that of his presence.

Carados strongly suspected that his amour was causing him to act. He told the king that it was necessary to surprise him, and that it would be easy to do so, since he was not suspicious.

That same night he went to the tower, when he believed that everyone there would be occupied in some celebration. He entered silently, and moved secretly, with the guards; he took possession of the Enchanter's person, and once he was captured his charms no longer had any virtue.

Isene the Beautiful was so frightened at first that she did not have the prudence to hide her passion, and a long faint completed its betrayal.

The Enchanter was taken before the king, who wanted to put him to death; but Carados represented to him that that punishment would be insufficient, and that it was necessary to torment him with an ignominious penalty. After he had thought hard about it, he opined that it was necessary to make him suffer in his amour, and that nothing would be crueler for him than to condemn him to the same destiny that the king had had. He was therefore given on three separate nights a slave, to whom a fay had given the resemblance of Isene the Beautiful. He could not protect himself from that trap, his knowledge and his art having become useless to him in the power of another.

He consoled himself in his dungeon, believing that he had the queen beside him, and that he was only suffering the rigors that she suffered, of which he believed himself to be the cause. After he had said the most sensitive, the most delicate and the most passionate things, the fay unmasked the slave. She appeared with her natural features; he knew his error and the deception to which he had been subjected.

Nothing can be compared to the dolor of the King of the Distant Isles; he was then released, but without making him promise not to see Isene the Beautiful again, that point—which was the most important—unfortunately having been forgotten.

He had been allowed to live in order to leave him the eternal shame of his infidelity; he sensed it keenly, and transported himself into the tower with Isene the

Beautiful, all of whose amiable company had been taken away.

He approached her, his complexion pale, his hair unkempt and his eyes lowered, without being able to utter anything but rapid sighs, which emerged with an expression of dolor that would have softened the heart of someone less interested in his pain than Isene the Beautiful. She looked at him sadly, and when he had recovered from his confusion, he told her with a thousand sobs of the torture to which his amour had been subjected. Isene paled in her turn, very keenly offended against the cruel Carados.

"Is it possible," she cried, "that he is our son? Let him die, I no longer know him. But no," she went on, "let him suffer as you have suffered."

After that they conferred, and the following day the queen summoned Carados, saying that she wanted to speak to him. He went to her immediately, and found her with her hair scattered; she told him that she had not expected him so soon, that she would make haste to have her hair done, but that he should open her cupboard and give her an ivory comb that had been sent to her from Rome.

Carados tried to obey, but scarcely had he reached out his hand than a snake bit him in the arm and coiled its body three times around it. The bite was so painful that Carados uttered a furious cry and fell to the ground.

The guards came running and took him to the palace. Expert surgeons were called, but they could not cure him, or detach the cruel snake from his arm.

The news of that accident soon spread everywhere, including the court of the god king, where everyone was in grief; but nothing was comparable to that of the beautiful Adelis, who departed immediately, with her brother Candor, to go to see her unfortunate lover.

She was on the way, while Carados was suffering vehement pains. He was in his bed, where nothing relieved him; he was languishing and withering under the rigor of his illness.

One evening, when he was more dejected than usual, someone came to tell him that a messenger had just arrived on the part of Adelis. He was troubled by those words, asked that the messenger should come in, but when he was beside him he turned his head to the wall in order that he should not see him so discomposed and so changed.

The messenger told him that Adelis and Candor would arrive the following day; he appeared to be satisfied by that and dismissed him. When he was alone he turned to his page and asked him to lock the door, after which he asked him whether he had a great deal of amity for him. The poor page, weeping, protested that he loved him so much that he would gave his life for him, if necessary.

Carados seemed slightly rejoiced by that assurance; he got dressed as best he could, ordered him to fetch his jewels and the tools that they might need; that done, they both went down into the garden and made a hole in the wall, which separated it from a forest. Carados worked himself, with his good arm.

When they were in the forest, they walked for three days without seeing anyone, nourishing themselves meagerly on whatever they could find. Finally, they perceived a hermitage, which was agreeably situated beside a little stream, with a pretty garden full of fruits and vegetables.

A white-clad hermit came out of the chapel. Carados went to him told him about his misfortune, of which the old man had already heard mention, and begged him to hide him and be good enough to allow him to spend the rest of his dolorous life with him.

The good hermit promised to keep his secret, and to buy two white habits for Carados and his page. He was so well hidden in that attire that no one knew him, not even the men that the king sent after him to search for him, who saw him and mistook him for a hermit.

Meanwhile, Candor and his sister arrived where they believed they would find Carados, and Adelis immediately went to the room where he dwelt. They found the door locked, and someone announced who it was that wanted to come in, but there was no reply.

The beautiful Adelis, surprised, spoke herself. "Open the door, friend," she said. "It's your Adelis who is here." Still there was no reply.

Finally, the impatient Candor had the door broken down, and they found no one, either in the bed or in the rom.

The most surprised was poor Adelis; she wept, she tore out her hair. Candor, seeing such a sharp dolor, swore never to cease traveling the country for two years, until he had found his good friend Carados.

He therefore went out into the world alone; he made enquiries everywhere he searched, but he did not obtain any news.

The time that he had prescribed for his quest gradually went by, and he came back, full of despair, to the realm of the king who was supposed to be Carados' father. He felt some consolation at the thought of seeing his sister again.

One day, he was in the forest, where there was a pleasant stream; he got down from his horse in order to rest and to avoid the great heat. He walked for some time in order to find a comfortable spot, and had found a very agreeable one when he heard the sound of a sad voice that was lamenting bitterly. He stopped, and was strangely surprised to discover, from the words that were being uttered, that it was Carados himself who was lamenting.

His joy was so great that he still suspected that he might be mistaken, but he advanced quietly, and saw a man dressed in white lying on the edge of the water. He would have thought, by the aspect of his habit, that he was a hermit, if he had not noticed the arm with the snake outside the sleeve.

At that sight, Candor uttered a loud cry and threw his arms recklessly around his friend's neck.

No confusion ever equaled that of Carados on seeing himself thus discovered; he wept with same and tenderness. Candor embraced him a thousand times without being able to speak; great joys are mute. Finally, they both recovered the power of speech, and they explained themselves like two friends who love one another sincerely.

After many legitimate reproaches on the part of Candor and poor excuses on the part of Carados, Candor obtained a promise from him that he would wait there, without fleeing as he had done before, and promised that he would return within six days.

After having obtained those assurances, the worthy King Candor quit his friend and went in all haste to see the king, from whom, without saying anything else, he asked permission to go and see Isene the Beautiful.

When he had it, he went up the tower and gave Isene a touching description of the wretched state in which he had found Carados. He implored her by virtue of the tenderness of blood, to forget the offense he had caused her and to cure him; and as he wanted to succeed in touching and persuading the queen, he even implored her by way of the Lord of the Distant Isles to grant him what he asked of her.

Isene the Beautiful had had time to appease her wrath. She replied to Candor that she would like to cure her son, but that the only remedy that there was appeared to her to be impossible, since it was necessary to find a virgin as constant as she was beautiful who was willing to suffer for Carados. After that, Isene told him the ceremony of the rest of the remedy.

Candor thought about it a little; and, having thanked the queen, he left her, and went to find the beautiful and sad Adelis. She was transported by joy at seeing her brother again; she asked him whether he had any news of Carados. He replied that he had found him, but in the most pitiful state in the world, and, finally, that there was also a remedy, but a difficult one, to cure him. She wanted to know urgently, what it was.

"My sister," he said, "it is necessary to find a virgin who has as much fidelity and beauty, who is willing to suffer for him."

"Ha!" she said. "Virgin I am; I am faithful; but as for beauty, I don't know if there's a sufficiency. But no matter," she continued, "let's try that which I have."

Then they gave all the necessary orders to have what was necessary taken to the hermitage, and the brother and the sister set forth.

When the beautiful Adelis appeared before her lover, he lowered his head, and covered his face to conceal his horrible change, which was such that the eye of a lover would not have been able to recognize him, had that circumstance arisen.

As soon as she saw him she ran to embrace him, and was so shocked that it was thought that she might die of it.

Finally, they told Carados a part of what was involved, for if he had known the risk to which Adelis was exposing herself, he loved her too much ever to have consented to it.

Large tubs were brought, one full of vinegar and the other full of milk, which were placed three feet apart. Carados had to set himself in the vinegar and Adelis in the milk. The princess hastened to undress Carados herself—that employment was very sweet for her—and when he was in the tub, she immediately climbed into the other. The snake that was on Carados' arm, which hated vinegar, was supposed to detach itself from his arm, leap into the milk, of which it was very fond, and stick itself to Adelis' breast.

Candor was between the two tubs, with his sword in the air, in order to strike the snake in mid-leap.

The faithful Adelis had the tip of her breast outside the tub, and called to the snake tenderly. Seeing that it was not coming quickly enough, according to her desires, she started to sing in a charming voice:

Serpent, see my nipples
Which are so tender and beautiful;
Serpent, see my breast
Which is whiter than hawthorn blossom.

At that pleasant song, the snake only made a single bound to hurl itself into the princess' tub, and gripped the tip of her breast. Candor was neither quick enough nor skillful enough, and, thinking to cut the snake in two, he chopped off the tip of his sister's breast along with its head. The snake died, but Adelis was in great peril; her blood had soon turned the milk crimson; she fainted, but the good hermit, who knew the virtue of simples, had soon put some on her wound, which stemmed the flow of blood. Not long afterwards, she was out of danger.

Carados was so touched by that spectacle that he did not feel the joy of his relief—every veritable lover would be similar—and he uttered horrible cries in his tub; but no one was listening to him. By the order of King Candor, he was put n a bath, as Isene the Beautiful had ordered. He emerged from it more handsome than he had ever been: in a word, the most charming of all men, and the most desirable for a lover.

In that state he went to present himself to Adelis, who could not thank sufficiently the good fortune that had delivered Carados from such a terrible evil. There were even circumstances in that cure that were of an infinite price and liking for Carados; few ladies would have had the qualities necessary to put an end to such an affliction.

The joy was great and soon spread all the way o the court of the good king, who made ready to come to the solemnity of the marriage of Carados and Adelis.

As soon as Carados had arrived at the home of the king whom he loved as his father, he asked for his mother's liberty. It was granted to him, and he flew to the tower full of joy, threw himself at her feet, begged her pardon, and took her to the king, who found her so charming that he decided to marry her again. But he only had the desire, for sudden death took the ability away from him.

Carados was crowned, and, the good king having arrived with the queen, the marriage of Carados and Adelis was made; there was nothing but magnificence, games and feasts. Isene the Beautiful was so beautiful there that it was suspected that she might have the advantage over Adelis.

An unknown knight won all the prizes and charmed the entire court by his fine appearance; he had a golden buckler, and, advancing toward the good king and King Carados, he told them that the buckle of his buckler had such a virtue that it replaced anything that was lacking, and that if it pleased Adelis to try it, it would restore the tip of her breast. She had some difficulty in making that resolution, out of modesty, but, Carados having undone the clasps of her robe, she caused the most beautiful breast in the world to appear. The unknown approached the buckle of his buckle to it, which immediately closed it, and a pretty golden nipple appeared on the queen's breast; she was known thereafter as the queen with the golden nipple.

The unknown knight revealed himself as the Lord of the Distant Isles, Carados' father, and he was fêted greatly. He asked for Isene the Beautiful for a wife, and she was granted to him. It was very just to recompense him for such a long amour, so ardent and so faithful. The four spouses lived in a perpetual happiness.

> *By different paths one arrives at happiness,*
> *Vice leads us there as well as honor;*
> *See as witness Isene the Beautiful,*
> *After merited torments*
> *She had a thousand prosperities.*

And the sage Adelis, so tender and faithful,
Long wrongly persecuted,
Finally enjoyed a similar fate.
Blind deity, excessively cruel fortune
Accord better that which comes from you;
Heap the wicked with eternal pain,
And give the virtuous the sweetest joy.

TOURBILLON

In olden times there was a king in the land of Armenia who found himself a widower, and, having lost a beautiful princess whom he loved tenderly, conceived a kind of aversion for all other women, and refused all the parties that were presented to him.

Uliciane, the queen of the marvelous promontory, celebrated for her beauty and even more for her science, made several futile efforts to oblige that king to marry her. She descended in a direct line from Ulysses and Circe, and the knowledge of that famous fay had come all the way to her from mother to mother.

She had her reasons for wanting to marry the King of Armenia; she had known from her books that a little daughter he had would be all the misfortune of her life, and would prevent her from being loved by the person she loved most in all the world. That knowledge obliged her to put everything to work to reach her goal; she only wanted to be Queen of Armenia in order to get her hands on Pretintin—that was the name of the little princess—and Uliciane knew that, if she could cause that child's death before she reached her fourth year, nothing would trouble the felicity of her amorous passion.

Is anything impossible for a fay—or, rather, a woman in love?

One day, Uliciane was in the forest where the king was hunting; she had a magnificent train, her flags were hoisted; they were shining with an extraordinary splendor. The king was very surprised by such an encounter, but he knew the customs of civility too well not to greet that princess. He found her beautiful, but he was insensible until the first morsel that he ate. She asked him to stop for a few moments in her tents; she made him a delicious meal, and the poor prince found himself caught and so charmed by Uliciane that he proposed marriage to her without further delay. She did not have to be begged, as one might imagine, and no marriage of that importance was ever made with less ceremony

It was not difficult for Uliciane to conserve the empire that she had over the king's mind. She caressed little Pretintin abundantly, who was passionately beloved by her father, and was the most lovable creature one could see. All the gifts of beauty were spread over her person.

She was approaching her fourth birthday; that was the term specified by destiny, and if she passed it, it would be fatal for Uliciane's amour. When the fay confided in her favorite, who was the minister of all her desires, and whose name was Arrogant, she gave him the little Armenian princess, ordered him to attach a stone round her neck and drown her, fearing that if he killed her in another way, there would be some mark of her demise.

Arrogant gladly took charge of such a commission. He took Pretintin and carried her to the vicinity of a river. He put her on the ground in order to look for a stone, and the charming caresses she gave him could not soften such a sanguinary nature.

Scarcely was she on the water's edge than a kind of storm blew up, with a great whirlwind, and when Arrogant wanted to take Pretintin in order to drown her, he no longer found her there, and searched for her in vain.

He convinced himself that the wind must have thrown her in the river and that the current had carried her away. He returned to Uliciane and told her that he had carried out her orders.

Meanwhile, little Pretintin found herself in a superb palace, where she was raised until the age of eight; but Uliciane, seeing that she was scarcely advancing in the joy of her amour, her lover only having loved her for a short time, was frightened to see that the certainty of her art had failed her for the first time in her life; her happiness was supposed to be founded in the death of Pretintin

She was very agitated by such an astonishing mistake; she consulted her books again, and, sensing her misfortune without comprehending it, she studied so hard and so well that she saw clearly that Pretintin could not be dead. She brought Arrogant back and, without intimidating him, tried to get the truth out of him by gentle persuasion,

He confessed everything to her and told her how it had happened, not knowing what had become of Pretintin. That confession was sufficient for her, and, having gone to consult the learned Proteus, she discovered that the princess of Armenia was in the power of her lover, but that she could only remove her from his palace by means of the handsomest young man in the world. Where was she to find him? That was what worried her. She set out on campaign, and asked one of her friends, who possessed the gifts of enchantment, to do the same.

It was done, and she discovered that the handsomest prince there had ever been was in France, Beauty was only a part of it, although it was charming; he also required thousands of perfections that would one day render him the marvel of the world.

Uliciane transported herself to Paris, and went all the way to the royal bed in order to abduct that handsome sleeping prince. He was ten years old; she took him to the vicinity of the palace where the lovable Pretintin was. The fay spread poppy juice throughout the enclosure except for the bedroom of the princess. Pretintin had the custom of sleeping late, and for the first time in her life she woke up as soon as daylight appeared.

Anxiously, she leapt out of bed and went all over the palace, where everything was peaceful. She went out, the doors being open and unguarded. She ran like a little madcap, and only stopped when she encountered a young prince as beautiful as she was. They looked at one another with joy shining in their eyes and held out their arms to one another as if they knew one another; they embraced, an already seemed to be forming a chain with their little arms that would attach them together for life.

After long caresses, the lovable children went for a walk on the sea shore; perceiving a little boat painted in all colors, they found it so pretty that, holding hands, thy leapt into it.

Scarcely was that light burden within the little boat than it set off at great speed, and had soon reached the cost of Armenia. The king and queen were in the port and received the lovable children. The queen claimed the merit with regard to her husband for the deliverance of the little princess, and, as he had been in despair over her loss he was delighted to recover her. He believed that he owed that entirely to the devotion of Uliciane, who had recovered her by means of her vast knowledge, so he confided the child to her. She made him believe that a new misfortune would threaten Pretintin if he did not leave her protection to her.

The queen had a palace built for her, which was only separated from her own by a garden, and it was there that she imprisoned Pretintin, whom she hated mortally, because of the indifference her lover had for her. She resolved to punish her for that by means of all imaginable tortures, and in order to make her sense them more keenly she was glad to light a vivid flame in the innocent hearts of Pretintin and the handsome Nireus, that being the name of the little prince.

There was in those young hearts a fatal preparation for what the fay desired; a foundation of infinite tenderness formed their characters. She wanted to afflict Pretintin in the person of her little lover, and was delighted that they loved one another recklessly, in order that she might make them suffer more subsequently.

She put the handsome Nireus under the protection of her favorite, Arrogant, and once a day he saw the princess of Armenia, because she knew full well that seeing one another and loving one another was the same thing for them, and she wanted them to see one another in order that they would love one another more.

That manner of procedure lasted until Pretintin was fifteen years old and the prince seventeen; they loved one another so much that no one could have loved any more.

The king was very annoyed at seeing his daughter so rarely; she only appeared on feast days and at splendid pleasures. Many kings asked for her for a wife, but they were always refused. The queen amused the king; she told him that the destiny of his crown was attached to that of his daughter, and she made up a hundred fanciful tales in that regard.

Once, when the handsome Nireus came to see young Pretintin, she found him sad, and knew that he had been weeping; the traces of tears were still on his beautiful cheeks, like the dew that one sees on flowers in the morning.

"What's the matter?" she said to him, with a natural urgency. "What's happened to you? Aren't you happy in my father's house? Do you lack something?"

"I see you," he replied, "and as long as I see you, I'm happy?"

"And how are you when you don't see me?"

"Until now," he said, "I thought about you when I didn't see you, and I was always content in thinking about you. But for a few days, Arrogant has been taking me every evening to a place known as the Deadly Isle. I find a monster there to combat, and I vanquish it. Those labors don't astonish me; I occupy my valor in that. My life is being rendered miserable by a thousand by a thousand indignities that I'd be ashamed to tell you, but the greatest of all my woes is that I'm threatened with not seeing you any longer."

That last phrase was punctuated by sobs; Nireus started to weep, and Pretintin could not help shedding tears.

She assured him firmly that she would speak to the king and the queen, and that she would beg them not to separate them; but the following day her despair was supreme when she did not see the handsome Nireus all day.

"Oh," she said, "It's over; I shall never see him again."

She did not want any supper and sent away all her handmaidens; she ordered that she be left alone, only being able to feel afflicted, and to think about what she could do in order to obtain news of Nireus. She had not been able to see the king, and the queen had scolded her for the concern she had shown.

What could she do, then? She was thinking and re-thinking, when she heard an impetuous wind; the windows in her apartment trembled in it, and those in her bedroom opened.

She was frightened, and was about to cry out, when she saw an extremely handsome young man come in. He was tall, of a surprising stature; he had a dazzling activity, a lively movement, in his eyes.

"I've come to offer you my services, beautiful princess," he said to her. "They won't be the first I've rendered you. Don't you recognize me?"

"No," she said to him, "I don't know who you are; and when I've seen you, I'll only remember Nireus."

"That's a frank confession," he said, "but I love you as much as Nireus does."

"What use is that to you?" she said.

"To love you," he replied, "without being overly chagrined. Don't you know that loving is the foremost of pleasures? I saw you one day in a public place. I saw that you were beautiful, and you pleased me so much that, although I'm naturally fickle, I thought that I'd love you for a long time."

"You seem to me to be singular in your impressions," she said, interrupting him. "May I not know who you are?"

"I'll satisfy you," he said. "I am Tourbillon,[18] of a nature almost entirely divine. My father is Zephyr; I was born of Flora, as a result of a clandestine marriage which my father made with one of the maids of honor of Prin-

---

[18] Turbulence, or, more specifically, whirlwind.

cess Felicity. Don't pay any heed to that fault in my birth; I'm nevertheless the son of a god.

"My father gave me the empire of the atmosphere, as he has, and, seeing me light and impetuous in my movements, he accommodated my fortune to my humor. My domination follows me everywhere, my palace is very beautiful, and I always carry it with me. My subjects, whom the vulgar name atoms and particles, govern the hearts of humans and link their inclinations. Don't be astonished if, having a people so gallant, I have such an amorous nature.

"You wouldn't believe how convenient it is to carry one's house and all its equipment like that. I change climates in accordance with the seasons, and I'm in a continual spring, sometimes on the summits of mountains, sometimes in the plains. I settle my palace in forests, or on the sea shore, when the whim takes me; I run from one pole to the other, I live for a while in India, I go to Asia, I fly to Europe, always making new amours; I only stop for as long as they last, and that's not very long.

"My estate, my palace and my subjects are invisible to mortals to the extent that it pleases me. What people call a dust storm envelops my entire empire, and that's why I've taken my name; when one of them is seen, it's because I'm transporting them from one place to another.

"I only appear with a bang; my approach is by no means secret. I like noise, and anyone who took away the racket that accompanies me would also take away my life. I come and go incessantly. Beauty attracts me; beautiful women like individuals of my character. I also have several children, who have all my bad qualities and none of the god ones, for if I'm fickle with regard to my mistresses, I'm not the same for my friends; I love them with attachment and I have nothing that isn't in their power; I serve them with an extreme vivacity. Those sorts of hearts are rare. I've already taken care of you, and it's me who stole you away from Uliciane's fury."

Then Tourbillon told her the story that I have already told, and Princess Pretintin, frightened by her stepmother's fury, seemed grateful for the obligations that she owed to the son of Zephyr.

"So the queen loves you," she continued, "but you no longer love her?"

"No," replied the prince of the air. "After favors little desired and too soon obtained, I abandoned her; but if you wish, I think that I might love you constantly."

"Oh, I beg you, let's not talk about amour," replied Pretintin. "I don't want yours; that if Nireus is all the charm of my life. Be my solid friend, you can still serve me against Uliciane's evil designs. But how can I call you to my aid, since one never knows where you are?"

"Here," he said, "is a talking trumpet. Even if I'm at the far end of the earth, call me, and I'll come. But only make use of it when necessary," he continued, "because, although this trumpet is only half a foot long, the sound it makes is so terrible that frightened people will fall down in terror on hearing it; Astolfo's horn was only a toy by comparison.[19] But if you wish, beautiful Pretintin, I'll remain beside you and protect you day and night; I have the secret of rendering myself invisible."

"Invisible!" she cried. How?"

"By putting my little finger in my mouth," he said, "and you shall know it."

---

[19] In Ariosto's *Orlando Furioso*, the knight Astolfo has a magical horn whose blast is so loud that it makes all his enemies flee in panic; he also rides a horse made of storm and flame.

As he said that, he disappeared, and Pretintin was frightened; then he had the audacity to steal a kiss, by which she was extremely irritated; she fled without knowing where.

"You're very bold," she said, "let me alone." And, extending her hands, she sensed that she was touching him. "Resume your figure," she continued. "Go away, so that I never see you; I no longer want your services; Nireus and I will be unhappy, I can see that clearly."

"No, my beautiful princess," he said, showing himself again, "I've just carried out my last function as a lover with regard to you, and since you don't want it, I'll only be a friend to you and Nireus. You'll see that I can give you sensible pleasures. I'll leave you, and I'll go to find one of the Mogul's wives, with whom I have a rendezvous on the stroke of midnight."

"I'll count on your amity, then," Pretintin said to him, "and I'm no longer annoyed. But can't you tell me where Nireus is, and what he's doing?"

"I don't know," said Tourbillon. "Tomorrow, when you open your window, you'll have news of him. Adieu; I wish you a good night."

Pretintin saw him depart, with some hope that he would oppose his power to that of Uliciane, and that he would bring her aid. She went to bed a little more tranquil, and slept better than she might have done; and in the morning, when she woke up, she ran to the window and opened it.

She was very astonished to see nothing there but three snowballs, with a drop of blood on each of them. She shivered, but, on considering them more closely she saw, in the drop of blood that was on the first, the Deadly Isle such as Nireus had depicted it for her; she saw him fighting a winged dragon, which he killed. In the second she saw the cruel Arrogant, who delivered him into the hands of Uliciane, who cast him into profound darkness. And in the third, the spilled blood formed these letters distinctly: *You have lost him for a year, no help can return him to you, be patient.*

The poor princess fainted on reading that. After she had come round, she wept for a long time, and resolved very meekly to follow the advice she had been given—which enraged the fay, when she saw her so tranquil.

It was true that Uliciane had taken Nireus away from the Deadly Isle, not for a year, but believing that he would be lost forever, which was her design. She took him very far away. Stopping between high mountains he showed him two roads.

"It's here," she told him, that we must separate. "Choose between these two paths. One leads to the Road of the Night, and if you take it, it's necessary to bring back the pillow of Morpheus and put it in my hands. The other leads to the Quarry of Day; if you follow it, you must bring me back one of the lashes of the eyelid of the Eye of the World."

Young Nireus smiled bitterly at the fay's command. "Rather ask for my death, Madame," he said to her. "Give it to me without so many complications and without amusing yourself by commanding me to do impossible things. What path do you want me to take?"

"The one that you wish," she said; and taking out a gold coin: "Heads or tails?"

It was quite indifferent to Nireus; the Road of Night fell to him.

Uliciane put a hand on his head, and he immediately found himself in obscurity.

He marched incessantly, but the night was perpetual. He lay down and went to sleep, but when he woke up

he could not see any light. He was hungry, he was convinced that he was doomed; he resolved, as a faithful
lover, to devote all his thoughts to Pretintin, while await-
ing his last moment.

He was not, however, so occupied with his passion
that he did not perceive a tiny glimmer, and when it
came closer, he saw that it was coming from a candle
that was held in the hand of a small boy, more agreeable
than Ganymede. He was however, a scullion; one sometimes sees princes uglier than a scullion, and this scullion was prettier than a prince, He was wearing a long
smock, in blue and gold cloth, with a very clean apron in
front, which was secured by two knots behind. He had a
red bonnet on his head, and pheasant's plumes behind
his ear. A golden ladle hung from his belt, and in his
hand he was holding a saucepan on the same metal. He
stopped beside Nireus and let him take a little broth,
which restored him marvelously; and he assured him that
he would see him every twenty-four hours.

Nireus wanted to question him, but, either because
the little boy did not like conversation or because he was
scared on that horrible road, he left him, and the prince
recommenced his journey.

He counted the days by the visits of the little scullion, and it was with a great joy that he found himself at
the end of the year.

He finally arrived in a large house, still dark, but illuminated by a few lamps. Nothing appeared to him to
be vaster than that dwelling. In the first apartments, such
bizarre things appeared to him, which changed and
changed again so promptly, that he realized that they
were dreams; he saw all kinds of them, and, still going
on, he found himself in the chamber of lovers; he recognized his face and he had the pleasure of hearing very

passionate speeches that he was making to Pretintin; he praised destiny, and it was a great consolation to him to think that his mistress was having dreams that were so favorable to him.

He paused agreeably in that place, but what a surprise it was for him when he saw Pretintin, so beautiful that he had never seen her more charming; she held out her hand to him, and he ran to her, utterly transported, but as he thought he was about to embrace her knees, he only found air, and she disappeared.

He searched for her for a long time and in several apartments, where he saw many things, each more extravagant than the others. Finally, he went into a very agreeable room and perceived a man on a bed, profoundly asleep, whose physiognomy was mild and placid.

He knew that it was Morpheus, whom the most unfortunate invoke and summon to their aid, and who suspends the rigor of the greatest woes. His coverlet was made of marmot skin, and he had a pillow of doves' down.

Young Nireus took that pillow, as the fay Uliciane had ordered him to do, and went out. Finally, he found himself outside the large house, and, wanting to continue his route in the darkness, he was opposed by a slight resistance. He went through it, and, perceiving the first light, he remarked a great imperceptible veil that separated night from day, and knew that he had, fortunately, passed through that slight interval.

He was overjoyed to see the light again, and it increased the further he went; he saluted Aurora, and had her first gaze; she considered him with pleasure, and thought him as beautiful as Cephalus.

Shortly thereafter, he found himself at the Sun's rise; he saw him emerging from the bosom of Thetis, and could not understand how he could bring himself to quit such a beautiful woman; but finally, after being magnificently dressed and having charged his head with brilliant rays, he mounted his chariot in order to begin his long excursion.

For some time Nireus followed the edge of the sea, and did not know what to do next, seeing that he was at the end of the Orient, when suddenly, he thought that the wind was rising, and a furious whirlwind passed over his head. The air having become calm again a moment later, he saw before him an exceedingly handsome young man. It was Tourbillon, who approached him with a smiling expression and asked him for news of his pilgrimage. Tourbillon told him that he was the one who had sent the little scullion to him, who had prevented him from dying of starvation, and that Uliciane, convinced that he was dead, was no longer thinking about him at all.

Nireus, who was naturally very good-natured, thanked him and asked about his origin.

Tourbillon satisfied his curiosity, and invited him into his palace, where they had the time to converse and to become friends. Tourbillon amused him tremendously with the narration of his gallant adventures, by the variety that there was in his amours, which his great lightness rendered temporary and of short duration. Nireus pleased him greatly, and they linked themselves together with a good amity.

Tourbillon told Nireus everything that had once happened between the Queen of Armenia and himself; that the unfortunate attachment of which he was the object, obliged her to torment Pretintin, because he had loved her a little; that she had sworn never to forgive her; that Uliciane knew full well that he could save one of the two from her fury, but had disposed the power of her art so cleverly that he could only save them both if the girdle of constellated metal that she wore between her skin and her chemise, to which all her charms were attached, could not be removed; and that, unless it was taken from her, one of the two would always be miserable.

The handsome Nireus sighed, and feared that at that moment the cruel fay might be doing some harm to Pretintin; the implored his dear Tourbillon to fly to her aid.

"She can't be suffering," he replied. "I've given her a little trumpet with which she can summon me, if she has need of me; but I understand you—you want to see her, and you're right; she's being punished enough by your absence."

Tourbillon rose up into the air impetuously and departed rapidly; he landed his palace at the end of the king's garden, very close to the one where the princess was being kept. To begin with he knocked down a section of wall and promptly made a door, which connected Nireus' apartment with Pretentin's.

The young princess was asleep when the two friends came into the room. It was summer and it was hot; the curtains of the bed were raised; she had one arm passed beneath her head and her other hand seemed to be retaining, modestly, the linen in which she was clad.

A candle next to the bed allowed her charming face to be seen. Nireus threw himself to his knees on one side the bed and Tourbillon went round to the other. Respectfully and tenderly, Nireus considered her placidly, almost without daring to draw nearer; Tourbillon, less circumspect, was carried away, took her hand with his usual liberty, kissed it, and woke her up with a start.

Her surprise made her shudder; on opening her eyes she only saw Nireus, more handsome than the son of Venus; she held out her hand to him, blushing. Turning her head, she saw Tourbillion, who, prompt in all things, told her in a few moments everything that had happened to Nireus.

She thanked the Prince of the Air for so many obligations; she heard with pleasure everything that her lover wanted to say to her, and responded to it as he wished.

Tourbillon, who rarely stayed for long in the same pace, told her that he would soon be leaving, that he would leave her Nireus, and that she should hide him among her handmaidens.

Pretintin could not consent to that, in all decency.

"Well, then," Tourbillon said to her, abruptly, wanting to favor her friend, "it's necessary that I take him back to the Deadly Isle or return him the Road of Night."

"What!" relied Pretintin, tenderly. "Do I only have those two extremities?"

Tourbillon was already smiling, and was about to propose a milder expedient, when he noticed that Pretintin was very frightened, on seeing Uliciane arrive in the room.

"I don't find you poorly accompanied," the fay said to her, "and you're spending your nights very agreeably." Her fury was extreme.

Tourbillon darted an imperious gaze at her, and jeered that she wished her nights were similar.

"It's not a time for laughing," murmured Pretintin, more dead than alive. "We're doomed."

But Tourbillon continued, in an excessive vivacity, which only irritated the amorous fay more. The handsome Nireus implored him in vain to calm down, with slight satisfaction. Tourbillon did not care, and drove

Uliciane to desperation with piquant darts, unable to constrain himself. Finally, he left, taking Nireus with him, and telling Pretintin that she knew the means of recalling him when the time came.

At that unexpected departure, Uliciane lost all patience; she went to find the king and gave him a monstrous account of his daughter's conduct, making him fear that she might be abducted again, and that he would also lose his crown, as she had predicted

The frightened king told her to do whatever she wished with Pretintin. Finding herself the absolute mistress, she took her to the Furious Isle and put her under the government of Arrogant.

What a fate for such a beautiful princess, so delicate and so neat, to find herself in such a horrible place! She was put in the hollow of a tree in the center of the isle and she was given a few roots and a few dates for her supper. All the birds of ill omen perched in the branches of that tree: the crows and the owls uttered funereal cries there and as soon as dawn broke, a malevolent owl let its droppings fall on Pretintin's head.

She suffered in such a sad state, consoled nevertheless by suffering alone, knowing that Nireus was safe, thanks to Tourbillon. Forgetting the sight of her present misery, she was thinking about her lover as tranquilly as if she had still been in her father's palace when, on looking around, she saw the fay, with Arrogant, who was holding a fatal noose in his hands, and two deformed dwarfs that were following them.

She suspected that it was her final hour, and that she was about to be killed. Although she was possessed of a considerable firmness of soul, she was very afraid, and a natural sentiment caused her to raise to her lips the little talking trumpet that she had in her pocket. She summoned Tourbillon with all her might.

The sound was so prodigious hat it caused a world-wide earthquake. A few cities collapsed; mountains fell; tigers and lions, which were as gentle in those days as dogs and lambs, became terrible thereafter.

Many people died of fright; the king of Armenia passed over, and the fay, who was not prepared for that event, fell unconscious. Arrogant and the dwarfs dropped dead, and, as the tree that Pretintin was in shook horribly, she perceived, with admiration, that it had all turned to gold, that its branches were all brilliant with various colored enamels, charged with luminous gems. The hollow that she inhabited was a beautiful chamber, embellished by all imaginable ornaments.

But nothing satisfied her as much as the sight of the handsome Nireus, and that of Tourbillon; she uttered a cry of joy. Tourbillon amused himself by joking about the fear into which the entire world had been plunged, but Nireus, enlightened by his amour, did not waste any time, and, seeing the profound unconsciousness of the fay, he put a bold hand under her skirts and unfastened the fatal girdle. Joyful at such a capture, he showed it to the princess.

Tourbillon, who praised him for his presence of mind, returned to his palace; he took the pillow of Morpheus and placed it gently under Ulciane's head.

"She will sleep," he said to Nireus, "until a daughter who will be born to you and Pretintin, who will be as beautiful as her mother, wakes her up and brings her out of it, possessed of as much generosity as she has had cruelty until now."

As he spoke, Tourbillon and Nireus carried the fay to the golden tree and put her in the magnificent chamber, with the pillow beneath her head; her girdle was hung from a branch of the tree, and the two dwarfs were paced with Arrogant at the entrance to the isle.

Uliciane reposed thus for a long time, and, the king of Armenia being dead, the beautiful Pretintin was crowned queen, and married the handsome Nireus. They owed their good fortune entirely to the obligations they had to their good friend Tourbillon.

> *Whatever faults are in you,*
> *One suffers them all gladly,*
> *If goodness of heart is shown fully;*
> *If you are able to help an unfortunate,*
> *And if you are generous,*
> *Without reflection or difficulty,*
> *A friend of such value is soon proven;*
> *Fortunate is the person who has found one!*

GREEN AND BLUE

There was once a queen who, finding herself pregnant, summoned one of her sisters, whose name was Sublime; she was a fay of profound and certain knowledge. She begged her to be present at her childbirth and to tell her the destiny of her child.

She gave birth to a little girl, whom the fay took in her arms; and, having considered her attentively, she saw in her physiognomy an extraordinary elevation, a nobility and a pride worthy of the blood from which she emerged; but she also remarked an infallible fatality if she loved an ordinary man. In a word, she knew that she would only be perfectly happy when she was united with someone lovable, but who would be entirely opposed to her, and that it could only happen after the accomplishment of several labors.

These predictions and these snags embarrassed the fay. She did not think that it would be easy to accomplish them. That opposition appeared to her to be an obstacle; she saw an even greater one in finding a perfect man; nature, already weakened in those days, only produced them any longer with difficulty, and extraordinary individuals were as rare then as they are nowadays.

The fay debated with herself for a few moments, in order to decide what she ought to do with the little princess, and, wanting to remove her absolutely from the reach of men, she put her, with her nurse and four princesses of her blood, who were the same age as her, in a cloud. It was there that she established her dwelling, so far from the earth and its corruptions that she hoped, with her care, to render her one day a complete young woman.

That princess had the most beautiful eyes in the world; they were blue, so animate and so vivid that the penetration of their gaze rendered the cloud the same color. From that it came about that the fay, in difficulty choosing a name to give her, called her Princess Blue.

Sublime gave her all her cares, to ensure that the soul of the princess was as beautiful as her body was perfect. She had the satisfaction of seeing her respond worthily to her hopes. Blue had the finest mind on earth; it was embellished with all the beautiful knowledge, and of the black science she knew nothing. She had as much reason as intelligence. The fay confided to her the fate that it was necessary for her to avoid. The pride of the princess impelled her naturally toward her fortunate destiny, and, found in her sentiments that it would not be easy for her to accommodate a prince like the majority of those that were to be found on earth.

That difficult taste pleased Sublime. She had not worked alone to give that singular lodgment to Princess Blue. There was a famous magician who was her intimate friend; malicious gossip asserted that there was something more, and that Thiphis—that as his name—had been in gallantry with her for a long time; what is certain is that they did not make a big thing without one another, that they communicated their designs to one another, and lived together very intimately.

Thiphis had a son named Zelindor, whom he had had with a queen that he had loved tenderly. That prince was so well made, and had so many fine qualities, that he already felt so much love for the princess that he saw her often, and Sublime sometimes believed that Zelindor might be the illustrious lover for whom she was destined; but she soon abandoned that thought, seeing nothing opposed between the two of them and not anticipating that there would be hitches to overcome if Thiphis and she had a desire to marry them to one another.

But let us leave those peaceful inhabitants of the air for a while; it is necessary to return to earth. Two years before the birth of Princess Blue, there was a young monarch who governed the whole world as much by virtue of his power as his mildness and his charms; even his beauty served to give him subjects. His name was Spring; the entire world was brightened up by his reign, everything flourished under his amiable empire, and he was loved to the point of adoration.

But destiny soon robbed the world of the charming Spring; there was a general morning over his loss. The queen, his wife, found herself pregnant when he died, and the philosophers, who regulated the course of the year and divided the seasons at that time, gave the name of that amiable king to the most agreeable of them, which has conserved the name of Spring ever since.

The queen gave birth to a son, who showed all the charms of his father from the very outset, which obliged her to call him Prince Green. His childhood was so cheerful and lively that he could only be represented in the brilliant charms of youth, and he was loved as much as the one who had given him life; he was entirely reminiscent of him, and no son was ever as worthy of his father.

His court was beautiful and gallant, but among the many beauties who sought ardently to conquer him, none had the glory of touching a sublime heart, which Amour nevertheless wanted to subjugate.

He emerged from a difficult victory, having just vanquished an old prince celebrated for his rigor, being a tyrant who laid all nature desolate. After that he only sought to relax in gallant celebrations and continual amusements

The rumor of his renown flew everywhere; he was not unknown to Thiphis and Sublime, who admired him like the rest. Zelindor was moved by a secret jealousy for all the praises that were lavished on him, and Princess Blue was even more stirred, unable to help thinking secretly that she was destined for such a charming prince and wishing that he was the one promised to her by destiny, at the peril of a thousand labors.

She abandoned herself to those thoughts, understanding fully that she would never love an ordinary man, and, as amiable and amorous as Zelindor appeared, when she compared him to what was said about Prince Green, she could only think of him as an ordinary man.

The fay Sublime read her secret thoughts, and approved of them; and as she was entirely proud of her courage and he great sentiments of which she was capable, she sometimes permitted her to descend on to the mountains, and from there into the plains, and to go hunting with the four princesses. She had even constructed an admirable fountain in a valley, in order that she could bathe when she was weary and wanted to refresh herself.

Princess Blue could even undertake longer excursions sometimes; she went into cities to see plays and other curious and amusing things. But as Sublime did not want anyone to see that prodigious beauty, she rendered her invisible by means of a veil that had the gift of concealing her from human eyes; that was the Veil of Illusion, which hides veritable things, and which often causes things to appear that are not. In fact, when Blue wanted to amuse herself, she put it over her head and had the four princesses hold the ends; she seemed immediately to take on the appearance she wished; sometimes she was a superb edifice, at other times a cabin, a clump of trees or an obelisk, in accordance with what she imagined, and in that way she went abroad in security.

One day, when she was visiting a park of marvelous beauty, she heard the sounds of a hunt; suddenly unfurling her mysterious veil, she wanted to appear as a statue of girasol, set upon four sapphire pillars. In that form she saw the whole hunt pass back and forth several times, and everyone was astonished by the marvel they beheld. Finally she saw a young man on horseback, in whom nature had deployed all her perfections. As soon as he directed his gaze at that beautiful work, he leapt lightly to the ground, and, having considered the statue for some time, which had all the features and all the charms of the princess, and resembled her so closely that one might have thought it animate, he knelt down quite bewildered.

"O God," he cried, "why is it necessary that this masterpiece comes from the hand of a man?"

The princess considered the young stranger with strange emotions; never had anything to charming appeared to her eyes; he was of an extraordinary grandeur, but his stature had an inexpressible beauty and seduction. His face was jovial and laughing, and the Graces had spread all their charms over him.

Blue lost herself in the examination of such a perfect man; she found a mortal poison for her heart therein.

Alas, she said to herself, *what if this is the man whose common qualities would render me unhappy? For*

106

the beauty of the person has no connection with the ornaments of the mind and the qualities of the soul.

That imagination did not last long, and she convinced herself that the interior must correspond with the exterior.

During these reflections, the prince was in a consideration so attentive that he had forgotten everything else. Then one of the young princesses proposed in a whisper to Blue that they be permitted to make a concert in order to complete his confusion.

The amiable Blue smiled, and told her that it was a good idea, whereupon the four princesses sang these words:

You see before your eyes the only thing that can charm,
The only object that one can love.
It presents glorious chains to your heart;
Amour has forged those precious bonds for you;
Hope, and remember that after long difficulties,
One can find a delectable fate.

At first the prince was so alarmed at hearing such beautiful voices emerge from the sapphire columns, in such accurate accord with all the dispositions that he then had in his heart to tenderness, that he did not know whether his condition was natural, in the presence of such a great prodigy, or whether he was still enchanted. Those words were repeated so often that he did not lose any of them, and allowed himself to be carried away by a flattering hope.

"What is it necessary to do," he cried, "to merit burning in those fires and hoping for the recompense?

What labors can astonish me? I will do more than Hercules."

A single voice replied to him:

Seek, and find the object that has been able to please you.

A second continued:

Persuade and please in your turn.

A third continued:

Let love be for your heart the principal affair.

The fourth concluded by singing:

Amour is the price of amour.

When those words ended, Blue, in concert with her princesses, disappeared, and her veil hid her from the eyes of the stranger, who remained in a sort of astonishment that approached stupidity.

"Where have you gone?" he cried, and stopped, utterly nonplussed. "What has become of you, divine figure, whose image has remained so vividly imprinted in my heart?" Then he continued: "But it's an illusion; some charm has formed what I have seen; am I in love with a statue, and can I hope to be the Pygmalion of my century?"

After many reflections, the poor prince appealed to his reason in vain; it could not help him; all that he was able to say about the chimera that he loved was that he loved her, and that fatal idea followed him and persecuted him everywhere.

Meanwhile, the lovable Blue was in no better state than him. She had only made the decision to quit him so abruptly and disappear from his sight because she saw that if she stayed any longer she might not be able to help showing herself to him in her natural form. Fleeing appeared to her to be a sure means of saving her glory and hiding a weakness to which she would have yielded in spite of all her courage.

She returned to her lofty abode with a rapid heartbeat whose origin she understood very well. *I'm yielding to my destiny, then*, she said to herself. *Is it good? Is it bad? I'm in love with a stranger, who might perhaps have no birth, and whose character might make me blush if I knew it. But no*, she went on, *if I can believe my heart, everything responds in him to such a beautiful representation; I cannot love anything that is not worthy of my love.*

Prince Zelindor presented himself to her as often as he could. The sight of him because insupportable to her; she treated him with such coldness that he despaired. She was naturally tender, and he could not understand how such a great change had come about. She became pensive, and, in consequence, solitary; he feared that she was preoccupied with someone, and resolved to observe her, often following in the footsteps of the princess at a distance.

She went hunting all day, and in the evening she went to the admirable fountain that the fay Sublime had made expressly for her. There were fresh waters that ran into a brilliant opal; the last rays of the sun seemed to pierce them in order to seek their abode there. The fire that radiated from Blue's eyes had an even more prodigious effect there; one might have thought that it was illuminating the water and setting the whole area ablaze. She bathed, and her beautiful body was only covered by a transparent undergarment. Her princesses were with her, and did what they could to cheer her up, her preoccupied mind only thinking about the lovable stranger.

But what joy and surprise she experienced when, while playing with her companions, she suddenly perceived him leaning against a tree, considering her with eyes full of amour.

It was Prince Green. Who else in the world could have done as he did? Hazard had brought him there, and his delight was extreme in finding the marvelous original of the beautiful statue he had seen, and which he had had in his imagination ever since. He was charmed to see that there was a young woman in the world made like the one he had seen. He flattered himself that she was not insensible to all the amour that he felt, and that, having searched everywhere and finally found her, the last lines that had been sung to him might have their accomplishment.

With that thought, he was considering avidly all the marvels that he had before his eyes when the princess perceived him. She had dived into the water; she raised herself up inconsiderately, without knowing what she was doing, and, by virtue of that, offered new beauties to the gaze of the amorous prince. The proportion and the beauty of that divine figure caused him such a tender transport that he could not help saying, impetuously, everything that he felt.

Blue could not hide herself; she no longer had the veil of illusion; it was on the ground with her clothes. To tell the truth, she was not sorry about that, and found some pleasure in the effect that her beauty produced.

There was even so much spirit in what the prince said to her, and his sentiments appeared so noble and so natural that the princess, by virtue of an instinct that is almost always reliable, did not doubt that he was the one to whom heaven had given birth for her happiness.

She wanted to respond to him with pride, but all she had was modesty. In asking him to leave her, she retained him by a passionate gesture; she wanted him to refrain from talking about amour any longer, but her gaze made him see that her heart was full of it.

Finally, he obeyed her, but he obtained as the price of his submission that she would permit him to find her in the same place on the following day.

When he had gone, the lovable Blue picked up her clothes in haste and lay down on the edge of the fountain while the princesses got dressed. She did not have time to dream, however; Zelindor approached her and let her know that he had been a witness to what had just happened.

She thought his indiscretion great and criticized it.

"Ah!" he said to her, "I'm losing you." And, as the penetration of a lover is extreme, he divined who his rival was.

"It's Prince Green," he said. "I have no doubt about it."

I suspected as much, said the princess to herself.

"You love him," he went on. "I saw that; but either I lack my father's power, or I'll be able to prevent another enjoying a wealth that Thiphis' cares have fully acquired for me."

He left her with those menacing words. The princess returned, firmly resolved to confide in the fay Sublime once she had seen the lover and was sure that it was Prince Green.

She foresaw that Zelindor would be at her rendez-vous the next day, and, addressing herself to a pelican that she loved dearly and which had a reasoning mind, it put the veil of illusion into its bosom, in the opening by means of which it gave nourishment to its young, and took it to the prince, in order that he could hide himself from his rival. He had gone to the fountain a long time before and was waiting there—an ordinary effect of the impatience of lovers. The pelican gave him the veil and told him how he ought to make use of it.

After that, Blue set forth and went to the fountain.

Prince Green ran to her as soon as he saw her in the distance, and spoke to her in the strongest, most tender and most passionate terms. The princess sat down on the ground; he took the form of a little flowering thorn-bush. He was on his knees next to Blue. He confessed that he was Prince Green. She told him, in her turn, that she was the daughter of the Queen of India. She told him everything that had happened to her since her birth, and the strange habitation that had been given to her to protect her from an inclination that might be deadly if it were not for a prince full of merit, but that it was necessary nevertheless that there should be some opposition between them.

Everything was equal between the two persons, and, seeing nothing opposed therein, they could not understand why they were not destined for one another, since they loved one another with so much passion already. Blue told him that she would speak to Sublime, not doubting that she would commit herself absolutely to their interests.

They swore an eternal fidelity to one another and separated.

Zelindor had gone to the fountain, and, not having seen his rival with the princess, he suspected some mystery. Not wanting to approach, he directed his steps in another direction, exactly that taken by Prince Green, who, not suspecting his misfortune, removed the veil of illusion and appeared uncovered to Zelindor's eyes.

Zelindor's fury was inexpressible; he knew, in consequence, the intelligence that existed between his rival and his mistress, and, full of the impetuous emotions of jealousy, he went to find Thiphis, whom he made party to all his woes.

Thiphis listened to them as an affectionate father, and shared them as a man capable of anything—which was an important point. He went without delay to make his complaints to the fay Sublime, who had just been informed by Princess Blue of everything regarding her.

He did not find her disposed to enter into his sentiments. They spoke to one another with so much heat that in the end they quit one another at odds, and separated. When Thiphis had proposed that the fay give Blue to Zelindor she had mocked him, and had replied that his son was not worthy to ask for the hand of a person of such perfection as Blue.

The rift between them being well established, therefore, each of them returned to their own home, and Princess Blue sent her faithful pelican to Prince Green again in order to inform him of everything that had happened and to tell him where he could see her.

They both went into a wood of musk-roses, in which every tree was surrounded by little jasmines; such a pleasant place seemed made to serve the felicity of the perfect lovers. They each perceived one another at the end of a prodigiously long pathway, and, launching themselves forward, they had both begun to run lightly when they felt themselves caught by the feet. Threads had emerged from the ground, which fixed them, without allowing them to proceed. They were still so far apart that, although they could see one another, they could not talk to one another—but it is everything, in an amour, to be able to see one another, when one cannot do any more. The unfortunate lovers made a hundred efforts to free themselves, and their gestures gave evidence enough of their dolor.

The four princesses felt themselves trapped in the same manner, and all that they could so was to deplore, with Blue, such an annoying adventure.

Night eventually fell; it was extraordinary that a person as important as Blue could spend it in that fashion, but it was necessary to resolve themselves to it, not without shedding tears.

Daylight returned, and as soon as it was light they perceived in mid-air a lovers' swing, the seat of which was magnificent and comfortable, and whose blue and gold silk ropes were sustained by four winged children. They stopped the swing, and Prince Zelindor got down, cut the lovable Blue's bonds and invited her to climb on to the seat. She tried to resist, but he put her there by force, and placed himself beside her.

What a dolor is was for her to quit the man she loved and go with the object of her aversion; and what a spectacle for Prince Green, who saw his rival abduct his mistress!

For the first time in her life she was separated from the four princesses; she bid them a very tender adieu, and those unfortunates pierced the air with their dolorous cries.

The swing rose up and stopped very close to the desolate Prince Green; and Zelindor, in order to add insult to is injury, sang these words:

Nothing is equal to my extreme amour,
Nothing is equal to my happiness:
Burst forth, transports of my heart,
I am going to possess the one I love.

The princess felt the blow with which Zelindor was striking Prince Green very keenly; drawing upon the aid of all the force of her amour, she said to him, through her tears:

I will always be faithful to you
Neither your rival nor death will extinguish my fires
Let us both love one another very tenderly;
Let us brave cruel fortune;
When two hearts are united in a mutual love,
There comes a time when they are happy.

She wept as she sang. It is since that time that operas have been written, in which the method is still used.

Surprised by such a fervent mark of amour, Zelindor caused his swing to depart, which did not stop until it reached Thiphis' superb palace. The gardens, especially, were marvelous; it was on their model that the ones at Versailles were made.

The princess was given pleasures every day, and those days, so agreeably diversified, would have been woven of gold and silk for a coquette, but the constant princess only found bitterness therein, and every day lasted a century for her in the presence of Zelindor and the absence of Prince Green.

Thiphis employed his cares to bend her in favor of his son and to convince her that he was the fortunate lover promised by destiny. He told her that it was unnecessary to search for a greater opposition than that of their hearts, since Zelindor's burned for her but her own was all ice for him.

"Oh, leave me alone," replied the princess. "What pitiful reasoning! Heaven promised me happiness by virtue of some opposition, but it is not in the heart that it was required. I can only be happy in loving as much as I am loved."

She lived sadly in that beautiful palace, while the fay Sublime, surprised not to see her return home, sent her pelican to look for her. It made so many tours that it arrived the day after Blue's departure in the pleasant wood where the prince and the four princesses were trapped. It broke the bonds that retained them with its beak and claws.

Prince Green embraced it a thousand times to thank it for his liberation, after which the bird quit him and returned the princesses to the fay Sublime. The prince said many fine things to them, and they to him, but it was necessary to part.

He emerged from the little wood and saw nothing before him but a prodigious plain, sterile and devoid of trees. He had only been walking for a short time when the sun, which was blazing, became extremely uncomfortable by virtue of its heat. Not having eaten for three days, he was almost in agony. He tried, therefore, to go back into the little wood in order to find some relief there, but he was unable to reach it; his steps, against his will, took him further into the frightful expanse that as so arid and uncomfortable.

He was suffering, and his torment was horrible; he needed his tender thoughts in order to arrest his furious designs, often having the desire to run his sword through his body.

In that frightful state, lifting his head toward the burning sun, he perceived all the air darkening without sensing any coolness, and he did not know what was happening, until, finally able to make the objects out, he saw an innumerable multitude of birds, of every species and all colors, from the phoenix to the wren. His messenger of good news, his dear pelican, was at the head of that legion; it stopped next to the prince, and at the same moment, the majority of the birds settled on the ground; the others remained in the air, and they all came together, tightly, to form a palace of a new structure.

The prince was very surprised; he went in by way of a marvelous portico. The apartments were variegated in a thousand different colors; the parquets were made of the egg-shells of all those birds, and the ceilings of the marvelous material with which they build their admirable nests.

It was in that prodigious dwelling that the fay Sublime made him sense how much power that she had over the air that had previously been the habitation of his dear princess; he was always served by the pelican and nourished with the most delicious dishes.

He thought incessantly about Princess Blue, and he had resolved to ask the pelican to search for where she might be when he saw a woman with a kind face arrive one day with the four princesses. He had no doubt that it was the fay Sublime; he threw himself at her feet; she approached him with a laughing face and made him a thousand caresses.

"I was despairing," she told him, "of putting an end to your woe and those of Princess Blue, Thiphis having a knowledge as great as mine; but I had studied your destiny so much that I finally learned that as soon as I discovered what the opposition is between the two of you, Thiphis' charms would be broken and I would only have to follow my pelican in order to find the princess, and then bring her back.

"I racked my brains fruitlessly searching for that opposition; I confess my stupidity; I didn't found it. For six months I lived anxiously, separated from a young woman I love so much, and who merits all the vivacity of my tenderness.

"One day, I went for a walk, full of sadness, and I stopped to consider the excellent economy of ants. There was one of those little republics, which was occupied in its ordinary labor. I was observing it with pleasure, when I perceived that they were making different figures and that their little bodies were joining together, forming these words distinctly:

It is in the names of those lovers
That the end of their torments will be found.

"I clapped my hands together in astonishment at that sight, and then burst out laughing. 'How stupid I am,' I cried, 'O human prudence, how blind you are! The simplest beings sometimes know more than scholars,'

"I admired a hundred times that such a little thing had embarrassed me for so long, in admitting that Green and Blue had always appeared to the vulgar to be incompatible colors;[20] but I hope to assemble them soon by the union of two persons who bear their names.

"Immediately, I came to find you," the fay continued, "And I beg you, let us not delay in going to Thiphis' home, where we will find Princess Blue."

"Will she still be faithful?" said he prince.

"I can assure you of it," said Sublime.

"Let's go, then," he said.

And when the judicious pelican took rapid flight, it was followed incontinently by the entre flying house, and they made the voyage promptly, which promised nothing but pleasure.

The palace stopped near that of Thiphis, the doors of which opened of their own accord. The fay Sublime entered without any obstacle, holding Prince Green by the hand and followed by the four princesses.

Thiphis, astonished to see them, did not know what to do or say. Princess Blue, who was dreaming at the edge of a fountain that was called Lancelade, hearing a noise, turned her head slowly, and, perceiving those she loved most in the world, stood up abruptly and ran toward then, transported by joy.

"I see you again, then," cried the prince, throwing himself at her feet, "And you see me again, faithful, as I promised you."

"The fay, who did not want to waste time in frivolous speeches or amuse herself with Zelindor's despair, took them back to their flying palace, which carried

---

[20] The popular saying "Blue and green should never be seen [unless there is something in between]" was till frequently recited in England in the first half of the twentieth century, but seems to have fallen into use since. There was presumably a similar saying in seventeenth-century France.

them to the home of the Queen of India, Princess Blue's mother.

What joy for her and what delight for the faithful lovers! Everything was gallant and superb in the celebrations, which went on for a long time.

On the day of their wedding, the fay Sublime gave them garments whose singularity was unparalleled; their enchanted clothes were made of thin herbs, sewn with blue hyacinths; their mantles were similar, lined with velvet moss of a nascent green. They appeared so beautiful in attire so simple and so lovely, which had so much rapport with their names, that people could not weary of admiring them. A thousand prayers were addressed to heaven for their prosperity; it was long and durable, because they always loved one another. Only the union of hears can make the happiness of life.

Something trivial separates lovers
They lose one another for lack of understanding.
In that condition, a tender heart
Steals away from happy moments.

This tale having been made for one of the greatest princes of Europe, he found it very agreeable, and Prince Green pleased him so much, that he gloried in bearing his name.[21]

---

[21] This reference is slightly enigmatic; it seems probable that the reference is to the prince of the blood, François-Louis de Bourbon, Prince de Conti, to whom La Force addressed the self-description cited in the introduction, but I cannot find any reference to associating him in a relevant fashion with the color *vert* [green].

THE LAND OF DELIGHTS

A king had a daughter beautiful in all perfection; she fell in love with a brave cavalier, the son of a king who was her father's enemy, and as she judged that such an inclination would not meet with approval she hid it carefully and resolved to marry her lover in secret.

Soon afterwards she found that she was pregnant; she feared the wrath of the king, for herself and for her child. She pretended to be indisposed, and in truth she was, but it was supposed to be a different illness. She remained shut away in her apartment, hardly allowing herself to be seen, only going for walks with a single confidante in the garden, at the far end of which there was a beautiful river.

The princess was in great difficulty regarding the care of the child that would be born; she did not want to confide its destiny to anyone and resolved to abandon it to the gods.

She gave birth to a prince, more handsome than Amour, and after having washed his face with her tears, under the spur of necessity, she put him very neatly in a cradle of Chinese wood, with the most beautiful lacquer in the world; she ornamented the child with jewels and precious linen, and ordered her confidante to set it adrift on the river.

That river flowed into the sea. The cradle was carried there rapidly and fortunately caught in a fisherman's nets. Surprised and delighted by such a miraculous encounter, he welcomed the beautiful child, had his wife nourish him, and enriched himself with his spoils. He named the prince Miracle, and brought him up with a great deal of care, but in the vulgarity of his profession.

He grew tall, so well formed and so handsome that he merited having another theater than the edge of the sea and another exercise than that of fisherman. He was incessantly busy with his nets or with his line and hooks, but he had eyes far more capable of catching hearts than everything he employed in catching fish.

He was approaching his twentieth year, and knew nothing other than his métier, although a natural instinct made him imagine that there was something better for him to do, when one morning, when he had all of his catch laid out on the sea shore, he had sufficient appetite to want to eat a few of the oysters he had caught.

They were excellent in that region, and that those of England could not have had such an exquisite taste. The prince ate some moderately, and, taking one that was larger than the others, as he had it in his hand and was raising his knife to it, it opened of its own accord and a voice emerged from it that made him tremble.

"Oh, my poor Miracle," sad that voice, "don't open me, don't destroy me, respect my shell, which is so beautiful and so polished."

The prince was frightened, and thought about dropping the oyster. "Don't be astonished," she said to him.[22] "Conserve my life, and give me liberty. Get back in your boat and sail to the big rock two hundred paces away; I

---

[22] *Huitre* [oyster] is a feminine noun in French, so the use of the pronoun *elle* in this regard could simple signify "it," but the oyster does give further evidence of femininity, and the potential sexual symbolism of opened mollusks is undoubtedly significant in this instance.

make my dwelling there, and I want you to put me back there; I promise you a fine recompense."

Miracle was humane; he leapt lightly into his little vessel, still holding the marvelous oyster.

"But who gave you the faculty of speech?" he said to it.

"In sum, my son," she said "there are great marvels; it's not important for you to know them; let it suffice that I render you in a brief interval an incomparable man. I only ask for a fortnight, during which you come to see me. You're charmingly handsome and you have the stature of a hero; I'll teach you all the sciences that a great prince ought to know. You're a prince too, don't believe that you're the son of a miserable fisherman; so you can render yourself worthy of reigning and you will reign if you abandon yourself to my guidance. Put me down there; that's my palace. Adieu, young Miracle, until tomorrow."

As you can imagine, Miracle was very surprised by so many astonishing things; he scarcely slept all night, and at daybreak, without considering whether the oyster might still be enjoying all the sweetness of slumber, he embarked and raced to his rock. He called out to her with all the lack of consideration of an impatient young man. A brilliant glare emerged from a concavity in the rock, and the oyster appeared.

In order to abridge my tale, I will simply say that he saw her for fifteen days in succession, and at the end of that time he was the most knowledgeable, the most polished and the most gallant prince on the world. He was ashamed to remember his first estate, and he begged the oyster to lead him to a great adventure.

"My son," she said to him, "I want you, by means of my advice, to acquire a kingdom, and render you the possessor of the most charming princess that there ever was; but the conquest of both must be made in a very singular manner.

"Listen to me; there is in the world a place that is called the Land of Delights; you didn't see it when I taught you geography because it isn't on the map; that's a mystery.

"You'll understand by the name of the country in question that it has all the beauties put together; let our imagination go, and it will still fall far short, unable to attain all the charms that the agreeable empire contains.

"The sovereign of those charming places is called Favor; she was born of the two most perfect lovers there ever were. The empire is scarcely populated, its inhabitants are like gods; the princess is divine. The land is a peninsula, only separated from that of Advances by a wall of milk that reaches all the way to the heavens. It doesn't seem to be anything, but it's everything, and bronze and iron are no stronger; even the birds have no communication from one realm to the other.

"There is also a princess in Advances, who does everything to receive those who try to land in the Land of Delights. One can only reach it by sea. That princess has a false appearance of Favor, and many people content themselves with her, thinking that she is Favor.

"The sea that surrounds almost all of the Land of Delights is full of adventurers seeking its fortunate shores, but it is very difficult to reach them, and few of those who are fortunate enough to arrive are able to stay there for very long.

"Take this coat," the oyster continued, "which is less superb than gallant; it's attached to this branch of coral. Here are fishing lines and hooks, and in this jar of ambergris you'll find your nourishment. Put all of this in your little boat, and let it drift. It will stop when the time comes, and when I believe you to be happy I'll go to see you. Adieu, my son."

The oyster went back into the rock, and the handsome Miracle put on his coat, picked up his jar and his lines, and let this boat drift at the whim of the winds and fortune.

After a few days' travel, on awakening one morning, it seemed to him that the air he was breathing was purer than usual. He perceived land, a land that caused some emotion in his heart. The trees there were tall and green; a thousand birds of rare plumage, whose song was harmonious, made the entire shore resound—but what a sight Miracle perceived over the sea! In the distance, he saw a superb fleet, which was that of a powerful emperor, who was making futile efforts to reach the Land of Delights. He saw magnificent ships that were also making little progress. He noticed many veiled women on some vessels, who were incognito, and could not land. He remarked an innumerable quantity of well made men who were attempting in vain to disembark in the charming country.

"Well, what can I do?" exclaimed Prince Miracle. "All alone? In what manner can I enter a land where I desire so passionately to be?"

His boat veered of its own accord and, taking a particular route, sailed on for another day. Having finally left all those vessels behind, very little was offered to his view when his boat stopped in a solitary and very pleasant place. Miracle did not know whether here ought to set foot ashore and whether he dared to disembark in that charming country. He fitted his hooks to his line and amused himself fishing while waiting until he had made a decision. As he was doing that, a slight noise made him turn his head; he perceived between some trees a person so charming that, by a true presentiment, he did not fail to guess that she was Favor. She was walking on her own.

"If you are not a goddess," the prince said to her, "you must be Favor."

"I am the person you have named," she replied, with a charming smile, and continued: "Have you made a good catch, agreeable fisherman? Cast your line."

The prince obeyed her, quite nonplussed, and when he withdrew it, all his hooks were charged with the rarest precious stones, of the finest workmanship. Favor was dazzled by them, and the prince was astonished; he threw them at the feet of the princess, and launched himself there at the same time.

"I aspire to other treasures," he told her, "and since being struck by the splendor of your charms, I can only love you."

"Many others love me," the princess replied. "I can only give myself to the most faithful; people are for a time, but not forever; that is why people only possess me imperfectly. It's still a great deal to enter into the Land of Delights; you're here, fear that you might not remain for long."

Having said that, she stepped away, in order to leave. The prince tried to follow her.

"I can't remain with you," she said to him.

She went away, and, the prince having tried to retain her, one of her ribbons remained in his hand. Her movement was so prompt and precipitate that, remaining fearful, unable to take a step, he cried: "Fickle Favor, you're flying away very quickly; I'm losing you at the movement when I have you."

With those words he found himself in a boat, and whatever he did, it was quite impossible for him to regain any port.

It was not the same boat that had brought him into that clime; it was cleaner and more comfortable. It had a little cabin with a bed, in order that he could repose when the fancy took him. Two young boys were guiding it, and were careful to give Miracle what was necessary to him. He had a new coat every day, an essential thing to please the majority of ladies. The prince knew that very well, so he took great care in adorning himself.

He spent a long time only seeing the Land of Delights and desiring the charming Favor, but that was all. He could not land. He thought he was able land there, but that was the realm of Advances. The queen was in the port, and from a distance he thought that she was Favor; he flew to her, and did not find any impediment. She received him in the most obliging manner, which was the last thing he expected.

He was very astonished, and understood his mistake.

"Oh, this isn't the divine Favor," he said, quite beside himself.

Advances was piqued, but it was not in her character to reject people. For Miracle she went as far as baseness, but she did not touch his heart. She had a certain air that sometimes appeared very charming; seen from certain angles she was very agreeable, but from others she was repulsive; she did not please persons of sensitive and delicate taste.

Prince Miracle soon quit that country and the queen; he went back to the little boat. The next day he received a sword-knot on the part of the queen of Advances; she continued to lavish presents in the following days, but did not satisfy him.

He was still searching for some favorable entry into the Land of Delights, and, as often happens, he found himself there when he least expected it. He only saw charming people, young and handsome; some were cheerful, while others concealed the most delicate contentment under a cold attitude. There were not many natural inhabitants, and it was rare for strangers to stay there for very long. The soil produced of its own accord, without the aid of art; there were no workers of any sort. Large storehouses of anything one might desire were found in that beautiful country. There were no cities to be seen there, but magnificent palaces, with gardens of an extraordinary beauty. Miracle could not approach the palace of Favor; there were many guards to get past; that of Caresses was at the door of his apartment.

He was well lodged, as one might imagine, but he only saw Favor in the distance. He was astonished to feel a perpetual spring in that charming land, but he was told that, as the most pleasant thing in the world that one does all the time becomes horribly tedious to the human mind and humor, which love diversity, there was an excessive heat in some parts of the country and an intense cold in others, in order to content the voluptuous. Young Miracle wanted to go there.

When he began to feel the heat, he saw superb tents on the edge of forests or in meadows, where one could savior freshness. Rivers of scented waters offered agreeable bathing, and everything that the human imagination has invented of the lively and the delicate was found there.

In the place where cold was dominant, there were large public squares where various spectacles were put on, beautiful palaces where balls were held, and private apartments with good fires of aloe wood. The candles providing illumination were made of those precious gums that are only found in Arabia, and the beds were aired by light embers of coriander seeds. There was no fear of the vapors in that land, their cause being unknown there.

Finally, the handsome Miracle was able to approach Favor; she made him envisage that she would give in to his perseverance if he continued to persuade her of his fidelity in such an appropriate manner.

He was not with her for long and, constrained once again to go back to his little boat, he wandered for a long time, and the castles in Spain that he built were his only consolation.

The favorable oyster that had helped him thus far was not an ordinary oyster; she had the same origin as Venus, having been born at the same time and in the same way; she reigned over the sea as the goddess did on land, and she was as powerful as her sister. She loved Miracle, whom she regarded as a child of the waters and whom she wanted to render happy; she disposed everything in his favor.

He entered the Land of Delights again; everything smiled on him this time. All the inhabitants came to him, with hats of roses on their heads, throwing flowers in his passage and perfuming his path, as was once done for Alexander the Great. He was not quite a great as him, but he was happier.

A thousand charming sounds were rising all the way to the skies when, though a crowd of agreeable people, he perceive Favor's caleche. This was how it was equipped:

The caleche was lined with a magnificent yellow fabric, quilted and padded and full of the rarest odors. The cinnamon of the ancients had not been forgotten. The curtains were in Spanish leather, attached with yellow and silver strings; by that color one can see clearly that the princess must be a brunette. The side glasses were made of a single diamond; there was none in front because Amour was the coachman and nothing must separate Favor from Amour. Enjoyment was beside that god, costumed as a slave, for he often treats her as such, although he obtains everything from her. Eight fine horses dusted with Cyprus powder drew Amour and his retinue; the Shepherd's Hour served as postillion, and the Pleasures preceded and followed the admirable caleche. Favor was sitting in it; she was leaning slightly on Modesty, who was beside her; the Graces were at the doors, and the prettiest between her knees.

The entire brilliant equipage stopped in front of the amiable Miracle; Modesty yielded her place to him, and Favor was his, by the command of Amour. Charming fruits were born of such a desired union. The prince was happy for the rest of his life always in delights, and always heaped with favors.

He died in extreme old age and his life only seemed a single moment to him at the hour of his death.

Favor devoted herself to others; she makes the felicity of mortals.

Fortunate whoever can obtain you,
Favor, caught by a faithful and tender heart;
You make yourself long-awaited
And very difficult to retain.

THE POWER OF AMOUR

Once, in Arabia Felix, there was a great magician. His son was named Panpan, Prince of Sabea. The secrets of his father's are could not give him anything acquired, because nature alone renders perfect, either for the charms of the person or for the gifts of the soul and the mind.

Panpan shone in society, at an age that did not separate him yet from childhood. He was the delight of all the eyes that gazed at him, and he bore the desire to love him into all hearts.

As he had a great fire in his intellect, and he was in a gallant court, his early youth was full of impetuosity. The transport of his senses guided his heart; he had as many mistresses as he saw beauties. No one put up a long resistance to him.

But Amour was not content with those frivolous conquests; he wanted to make another usage of a heart over which he wanted to obtain veritable rights.

The princess of Arabia Felix, whose name was Lantine, was born to subjugate him. Her person was so amiable and so gracious that one could not see her without sensing emotions that she alone was capable of inspiring. Her stature was not tall, but she was so relaxed, she walked and danced with so much grace, that her every action pleased. Her eyes were the throne of amour, or, rather, she did not have a gaze that was not a particular amour. The desire to please was the strongest of all her desires, with the consequence that she acquired coquettish mannerisms and became a coquette. Everyone around her loved her, and everyone hoped to be loved by her.

The Lord of the Fearsome Rock put himself in the ranks like all the others. He was an enchanter, who wanted to employ the force of his art to render himself the possessor of such a charming person. In order to succeed in his designs he linked himself with the fay Absolute, who had a great power over the fortunate princess; he abducted her and held her for a considerable time in a sort of captivity. Her charms and her mildness obliged him to render her some liberty. She saw her people again, and her presence brought back celebrations and games.

It was in those days that the young prince of Sabea saw the beautiful Lantine; to see her and to love her were the same thing, but he found his heart changed. It was no longer the fickle heart penetrated by so many different darts and so capable of taking the impression of all sorts of objects. His spirited sentiments became solid; the impetuous lightness passed, and all his fire was focused on the princess; from the moment that he loved her, he thought that he had never loved anyone but her.

That was not the only effect of the Power of Amour; the same miracle was produced in Lantine's soul, she no longer wanted to please anyone else; she knew that Prince Panpan loved her, and she loved him in her turn. She no longer had any desires except for him, and, enclosing herself in the pleasure of that conquest, she hated her charms when they continue to win hearts.

There was one day of the year that was destined to receive the tributes that so many princes made to the princess. They were all assembled at the foot of the throne, in a great hall full of courtiers. The princess and her retinue traversed it, mounted the throne, shone their momentarily and, stripping off, so to speak, an embarrassing majesty, went on her own into a magnificent cabinet, to which each of the illustrious tributaries was admitted, one after another.

They made her presents of an extraordinary magnificence and gallantry; and when it was the turn of the Price of Sabea, whom she had not seen until that moment, she had a surprise that she could not hide.

She saw a young man of agreeable stature and a face so charming that she gave him, with all her attention, the most sensible tenderness of her heart. He had regular features, large dark eyes, keen and passionate, a smiling mouth, beautiful teeth, a large quantity of curly brown hair planted with unparalleled charm on the top of his head, which made an extremely marked point that gave him a pleasing and singular physiognomy.

Panpan had already seen the princess, and was in love with her. He presented himself before her with boldly, but the first gaze she cast upon him humiliated him; he wanted to look at her but he did not dare; he lowered his head, knelt down before her and remained utterly nonplussed; his silence was long.

Finally, speaking in a timid voice, he said: "I have nothing to give you; you have everything when you have my heart, I bring you its homage; what the others give you is unworthy of you; what I offer you can only be offered to you."

"I accept it," the princess replied. "I scorn all the rest; be faithful."

The prince withdrew, in order to give way to those who had still to appear. He went out, his soul penetrated by amour; Lantine's was sharply attained by it.

The next day, the princess had the heap of beautiful and expensive things that she had been given gathered together. She made a trophy of them, which was secured with magnificent belts, on which four lines could be seen inscribed in letters of precious stones:

Superb rarities, presents so precious,
How contrary destiny is to you!
You are not what I cherish the most;
Yield to the only one that has pleased me.

The hopes of Prince Panpan were flattered marvelously by such a delicate confession, which no one else understood, but whose charm he knew. For some time he savored a perfect felicity in the tender and sensible manners of the Arabian princess—but she was, however, too lovable; could he be happy for long?

Jealousy began to torment him; he had as many rivals as he saw men. The fay Absolute often robbed him of the conversation of the princess; the Lord of the Fearsome Rock almost obsessed her, and a hundred others inconvenienced him by their assiduities.

He was in extreme difficulty with regard to letting Lantine know everything that was passing in his heart, but he had no intelligence with her. He was far from having his father's science; he regretted the death of that great enchanter, whose power would have helped him if necessary.

He became pensive and solitary. He retired at one time into an orangery; he picked up the verses of Anacreon, believing that reading such an agreeable poet would dissipate his chagrin momentarily, and leafed through them. He was only scanning them when he fell upon the third ode. That ingenious description of the arrival and the malice of Amour was occupying him with some pleasure, when a dazzling light struck his eyes and caused him to drop the book. When his sight was reassured he saw Amour himself as he is represented to us: a beautiful naked child armed with a torch, a bow and his arrows.

"What do I see?" cried Panpan. "Am I still reading or am I, in fact, seeing what I was reading?"

"You are seeing your master," Amour said to him. "You are seeing the lord of all nature; it is vain to regret the help that your father might have given you; if I favor you, your desires will be accomplished; I am the father of the fays and all enchanters; although I appear to be a child I have given birth to the greatest powers of the world; and such as you see me, I am the greatest sorcerer there has ever been."

"What use is all that," said Panpan, "if you don't want to do anything for me? I love Lantine, perhaps I'm loved; break the obstacles that separate us, unite us."

"You're going very rapidly, my cavalier," replied Amour. "You're only commencing the story of your life and you want to skip to the end. I sometimes go as quickly as you desire, but in your affair, destiny restricts my power a little, and I also confess, frankly, that I want to amuse myself a little by means of the diversity of the adventures through which I intend to lead you."

Panpan was about to implore him to abridge his difficulties and perhaps about to embarrass himself with a long speech. He had opened his mouth to begin when he saw that there was no longer anything there but a long streak of light and an arrow at his feet.

"Oh, sorcerer," he cried, as he got up, "who throws his charms into the depths of my heart, make their duration eternal by an abundant sequence of tenderness."

He believed that Amour would aid him. With that thought, he resolved to go to the palace where the beautiful princess was retained; he had the arrow that the little demon had left him in his hand. He was astonished to find advanced guard corps whose species surprised him. There was a row of marble statues, which all had their bows drawn. They unleashed their arrows as soon as he appeared, and he knew that he could not get any closer without his life being in evident peril. He stopped, as one might imagine, and tried to take another route, but similar archers were always ready.

The poor prince was frightened, and rightly judged that only the Lord of the Fearsome Rock could animate the very stones for his ruination.

"What can I do?" he said, utterly desolate. "I'll never vanquish those terrible warriors." He sighed, tormented himself, and did not know what to do.

Finally, he took it into his head to pronounce this invocation to Amour:

O you whose power extends all the way to hell.
Charming sorcerer, give me your science;
These obstacles are offered to me
To make me sense the power of jealousy;
I'm losing Lantine, I'll lose her
If I don't have your magical aid.

Scarcely had he pronounced those words than he felt very animated and he remembered the arrow he had in his hand; he thought that it was worth as much as the wand of the greatest fay, with the consequence that he launched it vigorously at the armed squadron. It touched all those phantoms, which, lowering their bows and putting one knee on the ground, opened their ranks and left a space through which the prince could pass. He picked up the virtuous arrow and advanced joyfully.

He traversed a park of marvelous beauty and had already discovered the palace so greatly desired when he perceived a palisade that rose up gradually, formed of tuberoses, carnations, hyacinths and jonquils.

"What's this?" Panpan exclaimed, slightly astonished. "This will only put up a feeble resistance." And, starting to laugh, he said rather cheerfully:

Charming sorcerer, I won't invoke you.
This obstacle isn't difficult'
To surmount it without you will be easy,
Flowers won't stop my stride.

As he spoke, he thought that a kick would knock down that palisade. He was alarmed to discover that it was firmer than a wall of bronze.

"I recognize the fay Absolute in this enchantment," he said. "These are her artifices, to forbid me the sight of my beautiful princess."

O you, he cried, *come quickly to my aid,*
Destroy this surprising mystery,
Dear master of my heart, protector of my days.
You're necessary to me again.

And, remembering his virtuous arrow, he presented its tip to that lovely palisade, which separated immediately, leaving him a perfumed passage.

The price of Sabea advanced, but, when he had nothing more than a flower bed to traverse, he saw it change into a lake of prodigious extent. He stopped, nonplussed, because he only thought of his arrow when he had invoked Amour. He put it on the ground, in order to detach a silken cord that held a little boat, and at the same time, the fay Absolute presented herself to him and picked up the arrow.

"Innocent," she said "do you forget your most powerful weapons thus? I, who know all its virtue, shall make use of it to harm you." Then she broke the frail piece of wood into a thousand fragments. "Combustible matter," she cried, throwing it into the lake, "have your effect."

Then, igniting of its own accord, the arrow produced a great fire, which consumed all the water in a moment; it remained hot and bright, raising its flames all the way to the sky.

The prince of Sabea was in despair at the stupidity he had committed in having abandoned the virtuous arrow; one only recognizes the mistakes one has made when one senses their prejudice. He stood there with his arms folded, considering the impetuosity of the flames, in a profound sadness.

"Do you want to set the world ablaze, cruel demon?" he said, finally. "These are your tricks: after the benefits you've allowed me to taste, you make me suffer the unbearable loss. You change in accordance with your nature, you abandon me and you turn to my disadvantage the very favors you had given me."

The young prince fell silent after those words and started to think with great application about what he could do to overcome his misfortune. Finally, he remembered that he had been living in flames since he loved Lantine, and that a fire ignited by the arrows of Amour could not offend his person.

"Perhaps," he continued, "those flames that seem so terrible to me are similar to the exaggerations of which lovers make use, in which I shall find far less than what I can see. At any rate, I'm risking very little; in the fury I'm in, I'd rather die than not see Lantine again.

As he finished speaking he threw himself head down into the fire. He thought he was in a delightful bath; he came and went within the flames with as much facility as if he had been in a garden. He felt a certain sensuality that delighted his senses; it seemed to him that he only lacked the presence of his dear princess, and he sometimes thought that he could do without that. He admitted privately that the pleasures of the imagination are often worth more than real pleasures.

While he was wallowing placidly in a place that ought to have been so hot, the princess of Arabia Felix was imprisoned in a palace by the cares of the fay Absolute and the jealousy of the Lord of the Fearsome Rock. She had no other company than that of her handmaidens, who tried hard to amuse her but did not always succeed. She had somber moments, and her natural gaiety was often lost in the memory that she had of the prince of Sabea.

One evening, she was all alone in her room, sitting by the fire with one foot on the grate, and her sight attached to an agreeable panting. She was turned away from it by an extraordinary crackling, which came from her fire. She looked in that direction; an infinite number of sparks emerged from it, which flew around her and attached themselves to her garments.

She was afraid of being burned and shook them urgently, but all the sparks surrounded her, and seemed to be playing in a hundred different fashions, buzzing like bees. Lantine soon became accustomed to that novelty, seeing that the fires had no malice. She found them rather pretty; they alighted on her face and all over her person, but whenever she tried to catch one they employed a great subtlety in escaping.

Finally, she captured one, but she felt an extraordinary tickling in her hand, with the consequence that she opened it promptly. Then they all assembled in the middle of the room, and when they suddenly dissipated, Lantine saw in their place a little old man who had a beard as big as himself; he had a fresh complexion, sharp eyes and a smiling expression.

She was not afraid, although that might seem strange; on the contrary, she approached him cheerfully.

"Father of all humans," she said to him, not believing that it was the truth, "by your long beard I suppose you to be such, where do you come from and what do you want?"

"I've just quit Panpan," he replied. "I want to unite you, if you abandon yourself to my guidance and do exactly what I tell you to do. You were right to name me as you did; I saw the infancy of the world; I am Amour."

"Amour!" cried Lantine. "Amour old and bearded! He's depicted so handsome and so young!"

"Don't you know any other?" he said "Here, I'll appear to your eyes as I did before Psyche." And, as he metamorphosed in the blink of an eye, she was surprised to see his beautiful form and marvelous beauty.

"Don't be astonished," he went on. "I can change as often and as promptly as the scenery at the Opéra."

"You're more than a fay, then," she replied.

"That's right," he retorted. "Their science is well below mine; my enchantments surpass all others; I'm the only true magician."

He told her then what he had done in Panpan's favor, and how he was keeping cool in the midst of flames.

"Would you like to come and find him?" he went on.

"I'm guarded in this place in too exact a manner," she replied. "I can't get out."

"Haven't I told you," he replied, "that I know more than anyone, and that I can upset all the designs of the Lord of the Fearsome Rock and the fay Absolute?"

"But decency doesn't allow me to go and find the prince of Sabea," she said. "It's more appropriate to bring him to me."

"Well," said Amour, "ornament yourself, and all your handmaidens too. I'll come to fetch you in two hours; I want to throw you a party, and I'll bring Panpan there."

With that, Amour separated from the princess

She summoned all her handmaidens and ordered them to go dress up; she even lent them all her jewels and told them to come and find her when they were fully decorated. Lantine changed her clothes and dressed in white, which was only agreeable in its simplicity; she coiffed herself with flowers, beautiful in her beauty alone.

When she was ready and her handmaidens had come back, she waited for Amour to appear. She was a little disconcerted to see the fay Absolute and the Lord of the Fearsome Rock arrive. That contretemps distressed her.

"Here you are, dressed up in a manner to conquer the whole world," the Lord of the Fearsome Rock said to her.

"Why the adornment of all your handmaidens?" the fay interrupted, abruptly. "Why are they like that?"

"To provide my sight with recreation," said Lantine. "I divert myself as best I can in the captivity in which you're keeping me."

"Well, Princess," retorted the enchanter, "I'm going to prepare a ball for you; you like dancing. As I can satisfy that desire, can I not similarly be the object of all the others you might have?"

"I've hurt my foot, milord," the princess replied. "It would be impossible for me to dance."

"Well, then," he said, "people will dance before you." Then, taking his wand and saying a few words, he offered his hand to Lantine and led her into a hall where there were a great many beauties and courtiers, with all the preparations for a magnificent fête.

Lantine sighed from time to time, and saw all of that apparatus without pleasure.

Some fête this is, she said to herself, *and how different from the one I thought I was going to have!* She felt a mortal ennui. It had only been a quarter of an hour since the ball had began when she thought that it had been a hundred years.

He chagrin appeared in her face. The fay noticed it and scolded her for it. Wanting to continue scolding, she opened her mouth to speak, but could only shut it again, and remained in that state, which surprised the princess slightly.

At the same time, the Lord of the Fearsome Rock was dancing, and, the woman who was dancing with him having finished the dance and returned to her seat, he danced on his own, and continued dancing, which caused not a little astonishment in the assembly. Lantine laughed like the others, unable to help herself. Then the violinists ceased playing; they went to sleep, and so did everyone else, except for the Lord of the Fearsome Rock, who did not stop dancing.

The princess of Arabia Felix, with all her hand-maidens, was conducted, without knowing by whom, into a vestibule, where a theater was rolling from the courtyard, and, when it reached her, she went into it with her handmaidens; it rose gently into the air and flew all the way to the bank of a beautiful river, where there were seats of incarnadine coral and a floor of halcyon plumes.

Nothing was as superb or as gallant as the decoration of that river; it seemed that cords of fire were hanging down from every star, and that at the required height they sustained a quantity of lights that formed different figures, which represented the attributes of Amour; Games and Laughs were playing various instruments, the Graces and the Pleasures were commencing the ball.

Princess Lantine was delighted to see such a charming spectacle, but by means of anxious gazes she testified that she would have liked something else. At that very moment she saw Amour and the Prince of Sabea, each as handsome as the other.

"You promised me," she said, with an expansion of joy that she could not hold back, "that nothing would be lacking at the fête you would give me."

"You're lucky," said Amour, "because I don't always keep my promises."

Panpan came to take the princess in order to dance, and they glided so gracefully over the surface of the waters that it was a marvel that they did not sink and that the frozen liquid had all the solidity required to sustain them.

The Prince of Sabea said a hundred pretty things to the princess, and she responded with at least as many.

After that, they were served an admirably good collation, and, Amour having presented Panpan with something to drink, the princess remarked that as soon as he had drunk it, he lost his reason; with the consequence that when the little sorcerer wanted to oblige her to drink it too, she refused. She was too prudent to risk putting herself in a shameful state, and, looking shrewdly at Amour, she sang:

> *Bacchus is rather dangerous, Amour,*
> *Don't mingle him with your charms or your fires;*
> *Stop, cruel divinity, stop.*
> *In that delicious and fresh wine,*
> *He's already dipped the tip of his dart,*
> *And its cruel venom goes from the heart to the*
head.

Amour started to laugh with Lantine and told him that there was not one woman in a thousand who would have had the strength to do what she had done. After that he judged that it was necessary to take her back. They put themselves in the same theater that had brought them, and returned to the palace of the fay Absolute. They found her in the same state in which they had left her, mouth open and asleep; the Lord of the Fearsome Rock was still dancing, and everyone else was asleep. They were amused at having made him dance for such a long time. Amour ordered that they should all be put in their beds, and it was done in a trice. He said good night to Lantine, and took her lover back to his house.

The next day, the fay and the enchanter thought that everything that had happened to them had only been a dream, so true is it that amorous adventures, once they have passed, have that appearance more than anything else. The enchanter found himself so weary that he could do no more, and felt horrible pains in the soles of his feet.

The fay, as was her custom, visited the whole palace. Her art did not inform her of the circumstances of the previous night because she had ceded to one greater than her own, but an indiscreet individual to whom Amour had done a bad turn told her everything that had happened. The fay was extremely angry, but not astonished, because that was the way Amour usually operated. She went to find the Lord of the Fearsome Rock and made him party to the whole story. He immediately resolved to go and find Amour and implore him not to oppose him any longer and to cease favoring Panpan.

With that design he made enquiries as to where the master enchanter might be, and having located him, went to see him.

"Lord," he said to him, "I know the trick you played on me yesterday evening. Have you resolved to steal Lantine from the tender amour that you have ignited in my heart?"

Amour started laughing, and admitted what he had done. The Lord of the Fearsome Rock begged him to wound Lantine in his favor, unless he preferred to render her fickle, declaring that he could not live happily while she preferred his rival.

Amour replied to him that he would not change anything in his organization, that he wanted the princes of Arabia Felix to belong to the Prince of Sabea, that he was not to importune him further, and should go away.

The Lord of the Fearsome Rock found that response as dry as it was, and felt it keenly, but he resolved privately to dissimulate. He thought that Amour had so many things to do that he could not always be occupied with Lantine and Panpan; that after all, he might have a few good moments; that between one enchanter and another there was only a turn of the hand, and that the lesser could often embarrass the greater.

Amour smiled, knowing what he was thinking; he dismissed him, resolved to quit everything rather than fail to devote the necessary time to the moves he wanted to make.

The Lord of the Fearsome Rock withdrew, and went to find the fay Absolute. He told her about the poor welcome he had received from the master of all sorcerers; they found themselves very embarrassed to know what they ought to do. Finally, they decided, judging that the simplest way would be the best to deceive everyone, even Amour.

In consequence, they gave their orders to return to the capital city, but as soon as they arrived there they transported the princess and some of her handmaidens to the palace they had just quit. There were subterranean vaults there of an admirable beauty, of which no one had any knowledge; the apartments therein were of an extraordinary magnificence. It was in one of those that Lantine was put. The enchanter lodged himself in the apartment next to hers, determined to guard her himself. No one is more vigilant than a jealous man.

The princess was somewhat afflicted to find herself in such limited company and in the power of her persecutor; she took it very badly, and would dearly have liked to see the little old man who had given her so much pleasure; left alone, she went into a cabinet, the door of which she closed behind her—and how surprised she was to find the Prince of Sabea there!

"Beautiful princess," he said to her, "I'm very happy to see you in my apartment."

"What!" she replied. "You're joking—I'm in Absolute's house."

"Amour has lodged me here," he replied. "I won't leave as long as you're here."

"But can I, in all decency, stay here with you?" she said to him

"You suffer the Lord of the Fearsome Rock here," he interjected.

"I can't prevent that," she went on.

"Do you want my death?" he retorted. "You only have to go and say that I'm here."

That powerful consideration obliged the princess to suffer what she could not prevent.

The time that they spent together seemed sweet to them, and when she went back into her bedroom her handmaidens put her to bed."

Several days went by in that fashion, so that they saw one another freely; but that liberty became insupportable to Panpan because he was no happier. He saw the princess, he loved her, he was loved by her; he would have liked to possess her entirely. One day, when he found Amour in a good mood, he begged him not to let him languish any longer, and to finish establishing his fortune.

Amour promised to content him; he summoned the fay Absolute to his presence and, in a moment, he turned her head, with the consequence that she consented to Panpan marrying Lantine.

Amour always torments, and always has someone who serves as the butt of his mischief; he wanted the Lord of the Fearsome Rock to be a spectator of the felicity of the prince of Sabea. He had him taken by Despair, who carried him away in a violent manner to the place destined for the union of the lovers.

147

The ceremony was to be held in a pleasant valley bordered by green hills and florid on each side. A gallant grotto, fitted out with everything imaginable of the most gracious—in sum, ornamented by the hands of Amour—was to serve as the nuptial chamber.

There were all sorts of amusements, and a comedy that represented the story of Venus. The supper was a beautiful as that of the wedding of Thetis, and although there was no fatal apple, there was an even more precious object on view, which as to bring as much good to the world as the apple caused harm.

As everyone was solely occupied in the pleasure of the good cheer, a clap of thunder was heard and brilliant flashes were seen; the heavens opened and a little lady descended therefrom, about eleven or twelve years old, formed with the utmost perfection. She was sustained by a woman whose face was mild and noble. That object was so full of majesty that the glare was almost unsustainable.

Amour appeared quite astonished; he was gripped by such great respect, accompanied by so much dread, that in an instant he had retired into his grotto with his entire retinue.

"Why that prompt retreat?" Lantine said to him; I see nothing more agreeable than that little lady and the woman sustaining her; tell me who she can be.

"She's the daughter of the heaven that Virtue governs," replied Amour. "She was given the earth to make her felicity."

"But why are you fleeing her?" asked Lantine. "What is there that is incompatible between the two of you?"

"I'm a spoiled child," he replied, "I'm not in a state to show myself before gazes so pure.

I always flee her presence;
Disorderly, libertine, living insensately,
Perfidious, unjust, self-interested,
Cruel and filled with inconstancy,
Can I stain the excellence of that object?

She, whose heart is formed
By modesty and nobility,
Whose mind is entirely animated
By the divine lessons that wisdom inspires?
Prudence guides her steps and actions.
Without knowing the passions
She has everything required to tame their caprices,
Hating and detesting vices,
Cherishing merit, loving virtues,
Innocence of mores is her fortunate share.

"She's an entirely divine daughter, then," exclaimed the princess of Arabia Felix, and you're just a rascal. It's a great marvel that you haven't led Panpan and me to our doom. I can see that there's a considerable hazard in the things in which you meddle, and although I find myself belonging very legitimately to the Prince of Sabea, it would have been better if this affair had been managed without your means.

"Now that I've seen that daughter of heaven, I have enlightenments that have never been presented to my mind, and I shall never counsel anyone to put themselves under your guidance.

For one fortunate amour under your empire
One sees a thousand unfortunate ones;
One ought to abhor your fires,

Never feel them, let alone speak them;
They spoil minds, and corrupt mores;
One cannot know tranquil joys,
As long as one is charged with your chains.
Who satisfies himself at the whim of his desires
Will only find that pleasures
Are less sensible than pains.

THE GOOD WOMAN

There was once a good woman, who had honesty, frankness and courage. She had felt all the disasters that are capable of agitating life.

She had been to the court and had experienced all the storms that are so ordinary there: treasons, perfidies, lack of good faith, loss of wealth, loss of friends. In consequence, reluctant to be in a place where dissimulation and hypocrisy have established their empire, and weary of a commerce in which hearts never show themselves as they are, she resolved to quit her homeland and go so far away that she could forget everything, and that no mention of her would ever be heard again.

When she thought she was far enough away, she found a small house in an extremely pleasant location. All that she was able to do was buy a small flock of sheep, whose milk would serve as her nourishment and their fleeces for her garments.

She had not been living long in that fashion when she found that she was happy. "It is therefore, an estate in life in which one can be content," she said to herself, "and by virtue of the choice I've made, I have nothing more to desire." Every day she spun with her distaff and guided her little flock; she would have liked sometimes to have company, but she feared the danger.

She had gradually became accustomed to the life she led when, one day, trying to bring back her flock, it spread out in the country and fled from her. It fled from her so well, in fact, that in very little time she could no longer see a single one of her sheep.

"Am I a hungry wolf?" she cried. "What does this marvel signify?"

And, calling to her most beloved ewe, it no longer recognized her voice; she ran after it.

"I could console myself for the loss of the whole flock," she said to it, "as long as you remain." But the ingrate persisted to the end and went away with the rest.

The good woman was very afflicted by her loss. "I no longer have anything," she cried. "Perhaps I won't find my garden and my little house in their place any longer."

She returned home quite slowly, because she was very tired after the running she had done. Fruits and vegetables nourished her for some time, along with a provision of cheese.

She was beginning to see the end of all those things. "Fortune," she said, "You can seek to persecute me, in the most remote places, but you can't prevent me from being ready to see the gates of death without fear, and after so much toil, I'll descend with tranquility into peaceful places."

She no longer had anything to spin, and she no longer had anything on which to live; and, leaning on her distaff, she took the path to a little wood. Looking around for a place to repose, she was very astonished to see three small children running toward hr, more beautiful than the finest day. She was pleased to see such a gracious company. They made her a hundred caresses, and when she sat down on the ground to receive them more comfortably, one passed his little arms around her neck, another hugged her from behind, and the third called her mother. She waited for a long time to see whether anyone would come to look for them, believing that whoever had brought them there would not fail to come and collect them, but the whole day passed without her seeing anyone.

She resolved to take them home and thought that heaven had sent her that little flock to replace the one she had lost. It was composed of two girls, who were only two or three years old, and a little boy who was about five. They each had little strings suspended around the neck, to which little jewels were attached. One was a golden cherry enameled with incarnadine, and around it was engraved the name Lirette. She thought that was the little girl's name. The other girl had a Mediterranean medlar on which Mirtis was written, and the little boy had an almond in fine green enamel, which had Finfin around it. The good woman understood that those were, indeed, their names.

The little girls had a few gems in their hair, more than enough to put the good woman at her ease. She had soon bought another flock and gave herself the comforts necessary to nourish her lovable family. She made them clothes of tree bark for the winter, and in summer they were dressed in white cotton cloth.

Small as they were, they guarded their flock; and this time, their flock was faithful to them, more docile and more obedient than the large dogs they had, which were gentle and kind to them.

They grew up visibly and spent their life in great innocence; they loved the good woman and she loved all three of them infinitely.

They occupied themselves in guarding their sheep; sometimes they fished with lines and extended nets to catch birds; they worked in the little garden they had, and employed their delicate hands in growing flowers.

They had a rose bush, which young Lirette liked very much; she watered it often, and took great care of it; she liked all flowers but thought nothing was as beautiful as a rose. Once, the desire took her to open a bud and she was occupied in seeking its heart when she pricked her finger on a thorn. The wound hurt her; she started to weep, and the handsome Finfin, who hardly ever quit her, having approached, also began to weep because of the pain she was feeling He took her little finger, squeezed it, and made the blood come out very gently.

The good woman, who saw their alarm over that wound, approached them, and, when she knew what had caused it she said: "What curiosity! Why spoil that flower, which you love so much?"

"I wanted its heart," said Lirette.

"Those desires are always deadly," the good woman replied.

"But Mother," said Lirette, "why does that flower, which is so beautiful and pleases me so much, have thorns?"

"To show you," said the good woman, "that it's necessary to mistrust most of the things that please our eyes, and that the most agreeable objects hide traps that can be mortal to us."

"So," said Lirette, "it isn't necessary to love everything that seems pleasant to us?"

"Undoubtedly not," said the good woman, "and it's necessary to be very wary of doing so."

"But I love my brother with all my heart," she said, "and he's so handsome and charming!"

"You can love your brother," her mother said, "but if he weren't your brother, you ought not to love him."

Lirette shook her head, and thought that rule very harsh.

Meanwhile Finfin was still occupied with her finger. He pressed the juice of rose leaves on the wound and wrapped it up. The good woman asked him why he was doing that.

"Because I believe that the remedy comes from the same source that caused the harm," he told her.

The good woman smiled at that reasoning. "My dear child," she replied, That's not so on this occasion."

"I believe that is in all cases," he said, "because sometimes, when Lirette looks at me, it troubles me entirely; I feel very disturbed, but a moment later, the same gaze gives me a pleasure that I can't describe to you. When she scolds me sometimes, I'm hurt, but when she finally says something tender, I feel joyful."

The good woman admired the way that the children were capable of thinking; she did not know what they were to one another, and feared that they might come to love one another too much. She would have liked to know whether they were siblings; her ignorance gave her a terrible anxiety. Their great youth reassured her.

Finfin was already full of concern for little Lirette; he liked her better than Mirtis. He had once given her some partridge chicks, the prettiest in the world, which he had caught. She had raised one of them, which had become an adult with fine plumage. Lirette loved it infinitely, and gave it to Finfin. It followed him everywhere, and he taught it lots of amusing things. He had once taken it with him when he was guarding the flock, and had lost it. He searched for it, extremely afflicted by the loss.

Mirtis tried to console him, but did not succeed. "My sister," he said, I'm in despair. Lirette will be upset, nothing you can say to me will diminish my sorrow."

"Well, my brother," she said to him, "we'll get up early tomorrow morning and well go look for another; I can't see you afflicted, as you are."

Lirette arrived as she was saying that and, having seen Finfin's chagrin, she started to smile. "My dear brother," she said to him, "we'll find another partridge; it's only the state in which I see you that gives me pain." Those words sufficed to bring serenity and calm back to Finfin's heart and face.

Why, he wondered, *wasn't Mirtis able to put my mind at rest with her generosity, when Lirette only had to say a single little word? Two of them are too many. Lirette is sufficient for me.*

On the other hand, Mirtis could see clearly that her brother made a distinction between her and Lirette. *Three of us aren't enough*, she said to herself. *I need another brother, who would love me as much as Finfin loves his sister.*

Lirette was already twelve years old, Mirtis thirteen and Finfin fifteen. One evening after supper, when they were all sitting outside their little house with the good woman, who was teaching them agreeable things, young Finfin, seeing Lirette playing with the jewel she had around her neck, asked his her mother what it was good for. She replied that she had found that they each had one when they had fallen into her hands.

"If mine wanted to do as I say," said Lirette, "I'd be very glad."

"Why, what do you want?" asked Finfin.

"You'll see," she said. Then, taking the end of her string she went on: "Little cherry, I'd like to have a fine house of roses."

At the same time, they heard a slight sound behind them. Mirtis was the first to turn round, and uttered a loud cry. She had reason to do so, for in the place of the good woman's little house appeared the most charming one that had ever been seen. It was not very high, the roof being covered with roses, in winter as in summer. They ran to it and went inside; they found agreeable apartments there, furnished with magnificence. In the middle of each room there was a rose bush, in full flower, in a precious vase; and in the first one they entered, they found Finfin's partridge, which flew on to his shoulder and made him a hundred caresses.

"Is it only necessary to wish?" said Mirtis. And, taking hold of her string, she went on: "Little medlar, give us a garden more beautiful than ours."

Scarcely had she finished speaking that one of extraordinary beauty was presented to their eyes, in which everything that can be imagined to content all the senses was found in the utmost perfection.

The children, immediately started running along the beautiful pathways, between the flower beds and around the fountains.

"Wish for something, my brother," Lirette said to him.

"But I only desire," he told her, "to be loved as much as I love you."

"Oh," she replied. "It's up to my heart to satisfy you; that doesn't depend on your almond."

"Well, then," said Finfin, "Almond, little almond, I'd like there to be a great forest nearby in which the king's son comes to hunt, and for him to fall in love with Mirtis."

"What have I done to you?" replied the beautiful girl. "I don't want to leave the innocent life that we lead."

"You're right, my child," the good woman said to her, "and I recognize your wisdom in such orderly sentiments. Then again, it's said that the king is cruel, and a usurper, that he killed the veritable king and his entire family; perhaps the son is no better than the father."

However, the good woman was astonished by the strange wishes of the miraculous children, and did not know what to think.

When night fell, she retired into the house of roses, and she learned the following day that there was a great forest not far from the house. It was a very fine place for hunting for our young shepherds; Finfin often went there to red deer hinds, fallow deer and roe deer. He gave a fawn whiter than snow to the beautiful Lirette; it followed her as the partridge followed Finfin, and when they were separated for a few moments they screeched for one another; it was the prettiest thing in the world.

The little troop lived together peacefully, occupying themselves with various exercises in accordance with the seasons. They always guarded their flock, but in the summer their occupations were milder. They mainly hunted in winter; they had bows and arrows and sometimes made long expeditions, after which they came back slowly and frozen to the house of roses.

The good woman welcomed them with a big fire; she did not know with which to begin in order to warm them up. "Lirette, my little Lirette," she said, "move your little feet closer," and, putting Mirtis in her bosom, she went on: "Mirtis, my child, give me your beautiful hands so that I can arm them; and you, Finfin, my son, come closer." And putting all three of them in a big bed, she rendered them cares that were very agreeable in their manner and affection.

They lived thus in charming peace. The good woman admired the sympathy that there was between Finfin and Lirette, for Mirtis was also beautiful and had qualities no less lovable, and yet it was obvious that Finfin did not love her as ardently.

"If they're siblings, as I believe," the good woman said, "what shall I make of their unparalleled beauty? They're so similar in everything that they're surely formed by the same blood. If that's so, that amity is very dangerous; if they aren't, I can render them legitimate by marrying them, and they all love me so much that their union would be the joy and repose of my days."

Given her ignorance, she had forbidden Lirette, who was already a little grown up, to be alone with Finfin, and she had ordered Mirtis always to be with them. Lirette obeyed her with an entire submission, and Mirtis also did what she had recommended. She had heard mention of a clever fay, and she decided to go and find her in order to enlighten herself as to the fate of the children.

One day, when Lirette was slightly indisposed, Mirtis and Finfin went hunting. The good woman thought that it was a convenient opportunity to go and find Madame Tu-Tu, that being the fay's name. She therefore left Lirette in the house of roses.

As she was going along her path she encountered Lirette's fawn, which was going toward the forest, at the same time she saw Finfin's partridge, which was coming in the opposite direction. They met up not far away from her. It was not without astonishment that she saw that each f them had a little ribbon around its neck with a piece of paper.

She called to the partridge, which flew to her, and, taking the paper, she found these lines thereon:

NOTE

Fly, dear partridge, go find Lirette.
I die a little when we are separated.
Paint her my ardor and my discreet pain.
Alas, I am almost assured
That such a perfect passion
Does not make itself felt in her hardened heart.
I would be content if Lirette
Could one day have a similar care.

"What words!" cried the good woman. "What expressions! Simple amity does not explain itself with so much fire."

And, stopping the fawn, which came to lick her hand, she detached its piece of paper, opened it, and found these words:

NOTE

The day will end and you still hunting;
Come back, amiable Finfin,
You left this morning
Before the break of dawn;
What absence, good God, will it never end?

"That's what people did when I was in society," the good woman went on. "How has Lirette learned it in this desert? How will I be able to cut the root of such a pernicious evil in good time?"

"What are you worried about, Madame?" said the partridge, then. "Let them be; those who are guiding them know better than you."

The good woman was utterly nonplussed; she knew perfectly well that the partridge as talking by virtue of a supernatural art. Fear caused her to drop the notes. The fawn and the partridge picked them up; one ran and the other flew; and the partridge called "Tu-Tu" so often that she thought that the powerful fay had enabled it to talk. She pulled herself together a little after that reflection, but, no longer having the strength to complete her little journey, she took the path back to the house of roses.

Meanwhile, Finfin and Mirtis had been hunting all day. Being tired, they had put their game on the ground and had lain down under a tree to rest. They fell asleep.

The king's son was also hunting in the forest that day. He became separated from his companions and came to the place where the two young shepherds were asleep. He considered them for some time with admiration. Finfin's head was resting on his bundle, and Mirtis had hers on Finfin's stomach.

The prince found her so beautiful that he dismounted from his horse precipitately and gazed at them with great attention. He judged by the small bags at their waist and the simplicity of their clothing that they were only shepherds. He sighed with dolor because he had already sighed with amour; that amour was even followed, instantly, by jealousy. The manner in which the young people were lying caused him to believe that such a familiarity could only come from the love that united them.

In that anxious thought, unable to suffer too long a slumber, he touched the handsome Finfin on the shoulder with his pike. Finfin woke up with a start and, seeing a man before him, he passed his hand over Mirtis' face and woke her up too, calling her his sister—a word that immediately reassured the young prince.

Mirtis got up, quite astonished; she had only ever seen Finfin. The young prince was the same age as her. He was superbly dressed and had a face full of charm.

He immediately said many tender things to her. She listened to them with a pleasure that she had not yet felt, and she responded to them in a naïve manner, full of grace.

Finfin saw that it was getting late, and the fawn had come to bring him its note; he told his sister that it was necessary to go.

"Come, my brother," she said to the young prince, holding out her hand to him. "Come with us to the house of roses." As she believed Finfin to be her brother, she thought that everyone as pretty as him must also be her brother.

The young prince did not have to be begged to go with her. Finfin loaded the game he had killed on to the fawn's back, and the handsome prince carried Mirtis' bow and bundle.

In that state they arrived at the house of roses. Lirette came to met them; she gave the prince a cheerful welcome, and, turning to Mirtis, said: "I'm glad that you've had such a successful hunt."

They all went to find the good woman, to whom the prince made known his birth. She took great care of such an illustrious guest, and gave him a fine lodging. He stayed with her for two or three days, which was enough to complete his flame for Mirtis, in accordance with what Finfin had asked of the little almond.

Meanwhile, the prince's servants had been astonished not to see him. They had found his horse and feared that some unfortunate accident might have happened to him. They searched everywhere, and the wicked king who was his father was in a great fury because he could not be found. The queen, his mother, who was virtuous, and the sister of the king that he had cruelly killed, was inconceivably grief-stricken at the loss of her son.

In her extreme affliction, she sent a message in secret to Madame Tu-Tu, who was an old friend, but whom she had not seen for a long time because the king hated her and had hacked someone she loved into bloody pieces.

Madame Tu-Tu came, without being seen, to the queen's cabinet. After they had embraced one another well—for there is not a great difference between a fay and a queen, having almost the same power—the fay Tu-Tu told her that she would see her son soon; she begged her not to be anxious, and not to take any chagrin from whatever might happen; that either she was much mistaken, or she could promise her a joy that she had not expected, and that she would one day be the happiest of all creatures.

The king's men made so many enquiries about the prince and searched for him with so much care that, having arrived at the house of roses, they found him.

They took him back to the king, who scolded him brutally, as if he had not been the handsomest young man in the world. He lived sadly with his father, thinking about the beautiful Mirtis. Finally, his chagrin appeared so evidently in his face that he was obliged to confide in his mother, the queen, who consoled him extremely.

"If you care to mount your beautiful hack," he said to her, "and come to the house of roses, you'll be charmed by what you see there."

The queen consented to that willingly; she took her son there, who was delighted to see his dear mistress again.

The queen was astonished by her great beauty, and that of Lirette and Finfin. She embraced them with as much tenderness as if they had all been her children, and conceived from that moment on a great amity for the good woman. She admired the house, the garden and all the singular things that she saw there.

When she returned, the king wanted her to render him an account of her journey. She did so, naturally. He was gripped by a strong desire to go and see so many marvels. His son asked him for permission to accompany him; he consented to that with an ill grace, because he never did anything with a good grace.

As soon as he saw the house of roses he coveted it. He did not care about the charming inhabitants of the beautiful place, and in order to begin taking possession of it, he said that he wanted to sleep there that night.

The good woman was very annoyed by such a resolution. She heard a racket and saw a disorder in her home that frightened her

"What will become of you," she cried, "happy tranquility that I savored? The slightest wind of fortune overturns all the calm of life."

She gave the king an excellent bed and retired to a corner of the house with her little family.

When the evil king was in bed it was impossible for him to sleep, and, opening his eyes, he saw a little old woman at the foot of his bed, who was no more than a cubit tall and who was also broad. She had large spectacles that covered her entire face, and was making frightful grimaces at him.

Cowards are subject to fear, and he had a frightful one; at the same time he felt a thousand needles piercing him all over. In such a great torment of body and mind he would be awake all night, and there were strange noises. The king ranted, and said words that were not at all beneficial to his dignity.

"Sleep, sleep, Sire," the partridge said to him, "or let us sleep. If the estate of royalty is filled with such anxieties, I'd rather be a partridge than a king."

Those words completed the fear of the king; he commanded that the partridge, which was reposing in a porcelain jar, be captured, but it fled when it heard that order and flew away, beating its wings upon his face.

He still had the same vision, and felt the same pricks; he was very frightened, and his anger became furious. "Ah," he said, "it's a spell of that witch they call the good woman. It's necessary that I rid myself of her and her entire race, and that I kill her."

He got up, no longer able to remain in her bed, and as soon as daylight appeared, he commanded his men-at-arms to seize all the members of the innocent little family and put them in dungeons; he had them brought before him, in order to witness their despair. Those charming faces, which were awash with tears, did not touch him; on the contrary, he obtained a malign joy from it.

His son, whose tender heart was torn by such a sad spectacle, could not look at Mirtis without feeling an incomparable dolor. A true lover, on such occasions, suffers more than the beloved person.

The poor innocents were seized, and they were already being taken away when young Finfin, who had no weapons with which to oppose those barbarians, suddenly took hold of the string around his neck.

"Little almond," he cried, "I would like us to be out of the king's power."

"With his greatest enemies, my dear cherry," Lirette continued.

"And that we take the handsome prince with us, my medlar," added Mirtis.

Scarcely had they proffered those words than they found themselves in a chariot with the prince, the partridge and the fawn, and, rising into the air, they had soon lost sight of the king and the house of roses.

As soon as Mirtis had made her wish, she repented of it; she knew full well that she had allowed herself to be carried away by an immediate impulse, of which she had not been the mistress; so, all through the journey she kept her eyes lowered and felt a great shame.

The good woman looked at her severely. "My daughter," she said, "you have not done well to separate the prince from his father; whatever injustice he has done, he ought not to quit him."

"Oh, Madame," replied the prince, "don't think it bad that I have the pleasure of going with you. I respect the king, my father, but I would have gone a hundred times over without the virtue, generosity and tenderness of the queen, my mother, which always retained me."

As he finished speaking they found themselves in front of a beautiful palace, where they got down. Madame Tu-Tu came to meet them. She was the prettiest person in the world, young, lively and cheerful. She made them a hundred courtesies and confessed to them that it was her who had made them all the pleasures they had in their life, and who had similarly given them the cherry, the medlar and the almond, whose virtue had had ended since she had them with her.

Addressing herself particularly to the prince, she told him that she had heard mention a thousand times of the displeasures that his father had caused him; that she warned him in advance that he should blame her for the bad things that might happen to him; that in truth she had played a few malicious tricks on him, but that was as far as her vengeance could go.

After that, she assured them that they would be very happy in her abode; that they would have flocks to guard, crooks, bows, arrows and fishing lines; that they would be able to amuse themselves in a hundred different pleasures. She gave them shepherds' clothing of infinite gentility, the prince as well as the others; their names and their mottos were on their crooks. That same evening the prince exchanged his oaths with that of the lovable Mirtis.

The following morning Madame Tu-Tu took them for the most charming walk in the world, and showed them fine pastures for their sheep and a fine terrain for hunting.

"In that direction," she said to them, "you can go as far as that beautiful river; never go to the other bank. In this direction, hunt in the woods, but be careful not to pass a large oak that is in the middle of the forest; it's very remarkable because it has roots and a trunk of iron. If you go any further, misfortunes might befall you from which I wouldn't be able to protect you, and afterwards, I might not be able to help you promptly, because a fay has many occupations."

The young shepherds assured her that they would do exactly what she prescribed, and started guiding their flock right away. Madame Tu-Tu remained with the good woman. She remarked some anxiety in her expression.

"What's the matter, Madame?" she said. "What doubt has risen in your mind?"

"I can't deny," said the good woman, "that I feel troubled leaving them all together like that. For some time I've seen, with chagrin, that Finfin and Lirette love one another more than is reasonable, and now, to add to that, another amity is forming; the prince and Mirtis don't hate one another, and I dread abandoning their youth to the drift of their hearts."

"You've raised those two young women so well," replied Madame Tu-Tu, "that you ought to have no fear; I'll answer for their goodness; I'll enlighten you as to their destiny."

She told her that Finfin was the son of the wicked king, the brother of the prince; that Mirtis and Lirette were sisters, and daughters of the late king whom the wicked one had killed, the brother of the queen whom the cruel king had married, and that they were therefore close relatives; that the wicked king, having mounted the throne, had committed a thousand horrors, and wanted to cap them all by killing the two little princesses; that the queen had done everything she could to stop him but could not succeed, and that she had called upon her help; that she had told the queen that she would save them. but that she could only do so if she also took her eldest son; that she had told her that she would see them all happy one day; that in those conditions, the queen had consent-ed to a separation that initially appeared harsh to her; that she had taken all three of them away and had con-fided them to the care of the good woman, as the person most worthy of that employment.

After that, the fay told her to rest easy, assuring her that the union of those young princes would render peace to the entire kingdom, where Finfin would reign with Lirette.

The good woman listened that entire speech with a great admiration, but not without shedding a few tears. Madame Tu-Tu was surprised by that and asked her why.

"Alas," she said, "I believe that they will lose their innocence because of the grandeur to which they will be elevated, and that so splendid a fortune will corrupt all their virtue."

"No," said the fay, "Have no fear of such a great misfortune; you have given them principles that are too good; one can be a king and an honest man. You know that there is one in the world who is the model of perfect monarchs; so calm your mind; I shall be with you as much as possible; I hope that you will not experience any ennui."

The good woman believed her, and after some time she felt a great satisfaction. The young shepherds also found themselves so content that they only desired a continuation of such an agreeable fortune. Their pleasures, although tranquil, were nevertheless keen; they saw one another every day, and the days still seemed too short to them.

The wicked king learned that they were in Madame Tu-Tu's abode, but all his power could not remove them from it. He knew all the dispositions of her charms; he could see that he would only be able to get them by means of cunning. He had not been able to live in the house of roses, because of the continual tricks that Madame Tutu played on him; he hated her even more for that, as well as the good woman, and that hatred even fell upon his son. He employed all sorts of stratagems to get his hands on any the four young shepherds, but his power and artifices did not extent over Madame Tu-Tu's land.

One unfortunate day—there are some that cannot be avoided—the amiable shepherds had taken their steps in the direction of the fatal oak. The beautiful Lirette perceived, in a tree twenty paces beyond it, a bird of such rare plumage that she had launched her arrow before even thinking about it, and, seeing the bird dead, she ran to pick it up.

All that was done rapidly and without reflection, with the consequence that poor Lirette delivered herself to her doom and was caught herself, for it was impossible for her to turn back, her will having become impotent.

She recognized her mistake, but all that she was able to do was to extend her arm pitifully toward her brothers and her sister. Mirtis began to weep and Finfin, without hesitation, ran to her.

"I want to doom myself with you," he cried, and in a moment, he had joined her.

Mirtis wanted to go after them, but the handsome prince retained her. "Let's go warn Madame Tu-Tu," he said. "That's the greatest help we can give them."

At the same time, they saw the wicked king's servants, who seized Lirette and Finfin; all that they could do on either side was cry adieu.

The king had had his hunters put the beautiful bird there in order to serve as a trap for the shepherds; he had anticipated the adventure that had occurred. Lirette and Finfin were taken before the cruel monarch; he made them a thousand insults and had them locked in a dark and strong prison. It was then that they regretted deeply that their little cherry and their little almond no longer had any virtue.

The fawn and the partridge came to find them; but the fawn, unable to see them, shed a few tears of dolor, and, seeing the king command that it should be captured and skinned alive, ran away back to Mirtis. The partridge was more fortunate; it saw them every day through the bars of their prison; fortunately, the king had not taken it into his head to separate them. When people are in love, it is a pleasure to suffer together.

The partridge flew back every day and went to give news of them to Madame Tu-Tu, the god woman and Mirtis. Mirtis was greatly afflicted, and without the handsome prince she would have been inconsolable. She resolved to write to the poor captives by way of the faithful partridge; she hung a little bottle of ink around its neck with some paper, and put a quill in its beak. Thus laden, the good partridge flew to the bars of the prison; it was a great joy to the young shepherds to see it again. Finfin put out his hand and took everything it had, after which they started to read.

MIRTIS AND THE PRINCE
to Lirette and Finfin.

Know that we are languishing
During such a long absence;
That we are sighing incessantly,
That perhaps we might die.
We might already have done so
If we no longer had hope;
We are sustaining our virtue
Since Madame Tu-Tu
Assures that you will live.
Lirette and Finfin, believe us
We shall see you in spite of everything,

And we shall have a pleasant fate.

That letter had a powerful effect on the spirits of Lirette ad Finfin; they conceived a great joy therefrom, and immediately made this reply:

LIRETTE AND FINFIN
to Mirtis and the Prince.

We have received your letter
With an extreme pleasure,
We have been able to feel it
More than we can express

In this place so full of horror,
Our torment would be extreme,
If we did not have the tenderness
That we encounter in one another.
With the object that is charming
One does not feel any torture;
And for those who are able to love
Everything can turn to delight.

Adieu handsome Prince, lovely Mirtus;
Have a mutual ardor,
Beneath a faithful tenderness
Always subjugated.

You have given us hope
To which we are sensible;
The greatest joy we could have
Would come from your presence.

Finfin attached that note to the neck of the partridge, which flew away rapidly. The young shepherds were consoled by the sight of it, but the good woman could not receive any since she had been separated by those persons so dear to her and whom she knew to be in such great peril.

"How my felicity has changed," she said to Madame Tu-Tu; "I am only in the world to be perpetually agitated. I thought I had made the sole decision that could put me in repose; how limited are the views one takes!"

"Do you not know," said the fay, "that there is no estate in life in which one can live happily?"

"I know that," exclaimed the good woman, sadly, "and if one cannot make one's happiness oneself, one rarely finds it elsewhere. But Madame, do something for the fate of my children, I beg you; I cannot live as anxiously as I am."

"They did not remember the order I had prescribed for then," said Madame Tu-Tu, "but let us think about the remedy."

Madame Tu-Tu went into the library with the good woman. She read almost all night long; and, having finally picked up a large book that she had often neglected, although it was covered in gold leaf, and she suddenly plunged into an excessive sadness. After a long time, at first light, the good woman, seeing a few tears falling on to the pages of the book, dared to take the liberty of asking her the cause of her dolor.

"I'm afflicted," she said, "by the irrevocable destiny that has just been offered to my knowledge; I shiver at it, and I tremble to tell you."

"Are they dead?" cried the god woman.

"No," Madame Tu-Tu went on, "but nothing can favor them unless you or I go to present herself to slake the vengeance of the king." The fay went on: "I confess the truth to you, Madame, that I do not feel enough amity for them, nor courage enough, to go and expose myself to such fury, and I believe that few people would be capable of doing so."

"Pardon me, Madame," replied the good woman, with great firmness, "I will go to find the king; nothing is difficult for me in order to save my children; I will give all the blood that I have in my veins, gladly."

Madame Tu-Tu could not admire such great resolution enough. She promised to do everything that was in her power to assist her, but she believed that she was limited in the matter by the fault they had committed. The good woman took her leave of her, and did not want to tell Mirtis or the prince what she intended, for fear of distressing and afflicting them.

She set forth, and the partridge flew beside her. When they passed the iron tree, the partridge removed a little of the moss that was around the trunk with its beak, and put it in the good woman's hands.

"When you are in the greatest peril you can be in," it said to her, "throw this moss at the king's feet."

The good woman remembered those words carefully, and, as soon as she had taken a few more steps, she was seized by the men that the wicked king always kept in the vicinity of Madame Tu-Tu's lands.

She was taken before him.

"I have you, then, wicked creature," he said to her. "I shall put you to death in the cruelest tortures."

"I've only come here for that," she replied, "And you can exercise your cruelty on me; spare my children, who are young and incapable of ever having offended you; here is my life, which I abandon to you."

All those who heard those words were penetrated with pity for such grandeur of soul; the king alone was unmoved by them. The queen, who was present, shed a torrent of tears; the king became indignant against her, and would have killed her if someone had not stepped between them. She ran away, uttering pitiful cries.

The barbaric king had the good woman imprisoned, and ordered that she be well nourished, in order to render a prompt death more frightful. He commanded that a pit be filed with vipers and snakes of all kinds, in order to take great pleasure in seeing the good woman hurled into it. What a genre of torture! How terrible it is!

The officers of the unjust king obeyed him with regret, and when they had acquitted that deadly mission, the king went to the place. They wanted to tie the good woman up, but she asked them to leave her free, assuring them that she had courage enough to go to her death in that fashion.

Considering that she had no time to spare, she approached the king and threw the moss at his feet. He was beside the frightful pit, and, as he wanted to consider it with pleasure, his feet slipped and he fell into it. Scarcely was he there than all the bloodthirsty beasts hurled themselves upon him, and killed him with their bites.

The good woman found herself in the company of her dear partridge, in the house of roses.

While these things were happening, Finfin and Lirette were almost dead of misery in their frightful prison, but their innocent affection was still keeping them alive. They were saying very sad and very touching things to one another, when they suddenly perceived the doors of their prison opening, and Mirtis, the handsome prince and Madame Tu-Tu, who threw their arms around their necks, were all talking at the same time, but nevertheless letting them understand in that disorder that the king was dead.

"He was your father, Finfin, as well as the prince's," Madame Tu-Tu said to him, "but he was unnatural, and a tyrant; he wanted to kill the queen a hundred times over. Let's go find her."

They went to her. Her virtue gave her a few regrets about the death of the king, her husband. Finfin and the prince also satisfied the duties of nature. Finfin was recognized as king, and Mirtis and Lirette as princesses. They all went together to the house of roses to see the generous god woman; she thought she would die of joy when she embraced them. They all told her that they owed their lives to her, and more than life, since they owed their happiness to her.

It was then that they believed themselves veritably happy. The marriages were celebrated with great pomp; King Finfin married Princes Lirette and Mirtis married the prince. When the fine celebrations were over, the good woman asked for permission to retire to the house of roses; they had a great deal of difficulty consenting to that, but they yielded to her desire. The widowed queen also wanted to live with her for the remainder of her life, and the partridge and the fawn also passed their days there. They were all repelled by society; they found tranquility in that retreat. Madame Tu-Tu often went to visit them, as well as the king and the queen, the prince and the princess.

Fortunate at those who can imitate
All that the good woman did;
Such grandeur of soul

Is more than deserving.

Cruel reefs, you can be avoided;
One scarcely fears shipwreck
When one can leave everything with courage.
Conduct, intellect, virtue, how much is owed to your
cares!
You appear among the necessities.

FRENCH CLASSIC FANTASY

Mme Barbot de Villeneuve. *The Naiads/Beauty & The Beast*
Chevalier de Béthune. *The World of Mercury*
Jean Carrère. *The End of Atlantis*
Félicien Champsaur. *Pharaoh's Wife*
Jacques Collin de Plancy. *Voyage to the Center of the Earth*
Gaston Danville. *The Perfume of Lust*
Paul Féval. *Anne of the Isles*
Charles de Fieux. *Lamékis*
Judith Gautier. *Isoline and the Serpent-Flower*
Nathalie Henneberg. *The Green Gods*
Gustave Kahn. *The Tale of Gold and Silence*
M.-J. L'Héritier de Villandon. *The Robe of Sincerity*
André Lichtenberger. *The Centaurs; The Children of the Crab*
Jean-Marc & Randy Lofficier. *The French Fantasy Treasury* (3 vols.)
Ch. Lomon & P.-B. Gheuzi. *The Last Days of Atlantis*
Maurice Magre. *The Marvelous Story of Claire d'Amour; The Call of the Beast; Priscilla of Alexandria; The Angel of Lust; The Mystery of the Tiger; The Poison of Goa; Lucifer; The Blood of Toulouse; The Albigensian Treasure; Jean de Fodoas; Melusine; The Brothers of the Virgin Gold*
Camille Mauclair. *The Virgin Orient*
Hippolyte Mettais. *Paris Before the Deluge*
Charles Nodier. *Trilby* * *The Crumb Fairy*
Edgar Quinet. *The Enchanter Merlin*
Henri de Régnier. *A Surfeit of Mirrors*
Restif de la Bretonne. *The Fay Ouroucoucou* (2 vols.)
J.-H. Rosny Aîné. *Pan's Flute*
Marie-Anne de Roumier-Robert. *The Voyage of Lord Seaton to the Seven Planets*
Nicolas Ségur. *Penelope's Secret*
Kurt Steiner. *Ortog*
C.-F. Tiphaigne de La Roche. *Amilec*

Simon Tyssot de Patot. *The Strange Voyages of Jacques Massé and Pierre de Mésange*